Palgrave Studies in Literature, Science and Medicine

Series Editors
Sharon Ruston
Department of English and Creative Writing
Lancaster University
Lancaster, UK

Alice Jenkins
School of Critical Studies
University of Glasgow
Glasgow, UK

Catherine Belling
Feinberg School of Medicine
Northwestern University
Chicago, IL, USA

Palgrave Studies in Literature, Science and Medicine is an exciting new series that focuses on one of the most vibrant and interdisciplinary areas in literary studies: the intersection of literature, science and medicine. Comprised of academic monographs, essay collections, and Palgrave Pivot books, the series will emphasize a historical approach to its subjects, in conjunction with a range of other theoretical approaches. The series will cover all aspects of this rich and varied field and is open to new and emerging topics as well as established ones.

Editorial Board
Steven Connor, Professor of English, University of Cambridge, UK
Lisa Diedrich, Associate Professor in Women's and Gender Studies, Stony Brook University, USA
Kate Hayles, Professor of English, Duke University, USA
Peter Middleton, Professor of English, University of Southampton, UK
Sally Shuttleworth, Professorial Fellow in English, St Anne's College, University of Oxford, UK
Susan Squier, Professor of Women's Studies and English, Pennsylvania State University, USA
Martin Willis, Professor of English, University of Westminster, UK

More information about this series at
http://www.palgrave.com/gp/series/14613

Arthur Rose · Stefanie Heine
Naya Tsentourou · Corinne Saunders
Peter Garratt

Reading Breath in Literature

Arthur Rose
Institute for Medical Humanities
Durham University
Durham, UK

Corinne Saunders
Department of English Studies
Durham University
Durham, UK

Stefanie Heine
Centre for Comparative Literature
University of Toronto
Toronto, ON, Canada

Peter Garratt
Department of English Studies
Durham University
Durham, UK

Naya Tsentourou
Department of English
University of Exeter
Cornwall, UK

Palgrave Studies in Literature, Science and Medicine
ISBN 978-3-319-99947-0   ISBN 978-3-319-99948-7 (eBook)
https://doi.org/10.1007/978-3-319-99948-7

Library of Congress Control Number: 2018957436

© The Editor(s) (if applicable) and The Author(s), under exclusive licence to Springer Nature Switzerland AG 2019. This book is an open access publication.
Open Access This book is licensed under the terms of the Creative Commons Attribution 4.0 International License (http://creativecommons.org/licenses/by/4.0/), which permits use, sharing, adaptation, distribution and reproduction in any medium or format, as long as you give appropriate credit to the original author(s) and the source, provide a link to the Creative Commons license and indicate if changes were made.
The images or other third party material in this book are included in the book's Creative Commons license, unless indicated otherwise in a credit line to the material. If material is not included in the book's Creative Commons license and your intended use is not permitted by statutory regulation or exceeds the permitted use, you will need to obtain permission directly from the copyright holder.
The use of general descriptive names, registered names, trademarks, service marks, etc. in this publication does not imply, even in the absence of a specific statement, that such names are exempt from the relevant protective laws and regulations and therefore free for general use.
The publisher, the authors and the editors are safe to assume that the advice and information in this book are believed to be true and accurate at the date of publication. Neither the publisher nor the authors or the editors give a warranty, express or implied, with respect to the material contained herein or for any errors or omissions that may have been made. The publisher remains neutral with regard to jurisdictional claims in published maps and institutional affiliations.

Cover illustration: © Melisa Hasan

This Palgrave Pivot imprint is published by the registered company Springer Nature Switzerland AG
The registered company address is: Gewerbestrasse 11, 6330 Cham, Switzerland

Acknowledgements

This book originally emerged as a panel discussion organised by Naya Tsentourou for the 2016 Annual Conference of the British Society of Literature and Science at the University of Birmingham. The authors would like to thank Ben Doyle and Milly Davies at Palgrave for all their support and patience as this project developed. Rose and Saunders were supported by the Wellcome Trust Senior Investigator Award Life of Breath (103339/Z/13/Z). Saunders and Garratt were supported by the Wellcome Trust Collaborative Award Hearing the Voice (108720/Z/13/Z). Heine was supported by a Swiss National Foundation (SNF) Postdoc.Mobility Fellowship. The contributors thank the Wellcome Trust for supporting the publication of this work as an Open Access volume.

Contents

1. Introduction: Reading Breath in Literature   1
   Arthur Rose

2. The Play of Breath: Chaucer's Narratives of Feeling   17
   Corinne Saunders

3. Wasting Breath in *Hamlet*   39
   Naya Tsentourou

4. Out of Breath: Respiratory Aesthetics from Ruskin to Vernon Lee   65
   Peter Garratt

5. Ebb and Flow: Breath-Writing from Ancient Rhetoric to Jack Kerouac and Allen Ginsberg   91
   Stefanie Heine

6. Combat Breathing in Salman Rushdie's *The Moor's Last Sigh*   113
   Arthur Rose

Authors and Contributors

Peter Garratt is Associate Professor in the Department of English Studies at Durham University. His publications include *Victorian Empiricism* (2010) and *The Cognitive Humanities: Embodied Mind in Literature and Culture* (2016). A forthcoming volume, *Distributed Cognition from Victorian Culture to Modernism*, co-edited with Miranda Anderson and Mark Sprevak, will be published in late 2018.

Stefanie Heine is a Postdoctoral Fellow (SNF Postdoc.Mobility) at the Centre for Comparative Literature at the University of Toronto, Canada. She is the author of *Visible Words and Chromatic Pulse. Virginia Woolf's Writing, Impressionist Painting, Maurice Blanchot's Image* (2014).

Arthur Rose is Postdoctoral Research Fellow in English Studies and Medical Humanities at Durham University, UK. He is author of *Literary Cynics: Borges, Beckett, Coetzee* (2017) and co-edited, with Michael J. Kelly, *Theories of History: History Read across the Humanities* (2018).

Corinne Saunders is Professor of Medieval Literature and Co-Director of the Institute of Medical Humanities, Durham University. Her publications include *Magic and the Supernatural in Medieval English Romance* (2010) and (co-edited with Carolyne Larrington and Frank Brandsma) *Emotions in Medieval Arthurian Literature: Body, Mind, Voice* (2015).

Naya Tsentourou is Lecturer in Early Modern Literature at the University of Exeter, Penryn. She is the author of *Milton and the Early Modern Culture of Devotion: Bodies at Prayer* (2017) and has co-edited, with Lucia Nigri, *Forms of Hypocrisy in Early Modern England* (2017).

CHAPTER 1

Introduction: Reading Breath in Literature

Arthur Rose

Abstract This chapter presents current debates around breathing and breathlessness in the medical humanities and frames this collection of essays as a series of interventions that attend to literature's role in such debates. Specifically, these essays consider what literature might offer to discussions of breath as a phenomenon that blends physiology with culturally rich metaphors.

Keywords Breath · Medical humanities · Markedness · Embodied poetics · Literature

Breath is an autonomic function that is essential for life. Luce Irigaray writes, in "The Age of Breath," "breathing, in fact, corresponds to the first autonomous gesture of a human being."[1] In a less anthropocentric, more physiological sense, breath, as a term, catches and brings together all those processes by which beings with lungs take in and release air: the mechanical, the chemical, the affective and the metaphoric. The diaphragm contracts. It drops. A vacuum appears in the chest cavity, which allows the lungs to expand with air. While the lungs are surfeit with air, oxygen passes through thin membranes in the alveoli to bond with haemoglobin, which, in turn, releases its load of carbon dioxide. The experience can be ecstatic, as for Keri Hulme in this description of breathing

© The Author(s) 2019
A. Rose et al., *Reading Breath in Literature*,
Palgrave Studies in Literature, Science and Medicine,
https://doi.org/10.1007/978-3-319-99948-7_1

from *Te Kaihau/The Windeater*: "It was ecstasy, it was *sweet*, air soughing in and all my little alveoli singing away with joy and oxygen-energy coursing through every space and particle of me."[2] It may also be deeply distressing, as in this passage by Michael Symmons Roberts in *Breath*:

> Baras closes his eyes and tries to settle his breath into a slower, deeper rhythm. Ever since his lungs were damaged, he has found it hard to see it as a failure of his own body. Somehow now on the brink of having his weakest lung cut out and replaced with a new one, he can't locate the problem in his own chest. Sure his chest is heaving as his lungs try to drag in the air, but it still feels like a problem with the air, not with his own body. On that April morning so many years ago the air itself was altered, and his sensitive lungs failed to adapt. ... His lungs were designed to take the cream off the thick air, and now the cream has gone he cannot recalibrate.[3]

For Hulme's narrator, breath brings a heightened bodily connection to her environment. Baras's breathing, on the other hand, seems to alienate him from his environment. Yet, in both descriptions, a clear interest in the mechanical and the chemical aspects of breathing is subordinated to figurative language. For Hulme, this figurative language emerges in the verbs she chooses: breath "soughs" like the wind, "sings" like the voice, "courses" like water. Baras finds similar expression in metaphor: "His lungs were designed to take the cream off the thick air." Literary representations of breathing like these, whether pleasant or unpleasant, demonstrate a grammar at work in thinking and writing about breath. This book responds to this implicit demand for a grammar of breath by developing, through five case studies, methodologies for considering breath in the literary medical humanities.

Literature in the medical humanities no longer simply offers a narrative supplement to medical insights. Narrative medicine, in its traditional iterations, prioritised literature's potential to build empathy and understanding of the patient's experiences.[4] More recent work has suggested that literature, and other such disciplines, might intervene more directly. Viney et al., for instance, focus on "intervention" explicitly: "Can the medical humanities intervene more explicitly in ontological questions—in particular, of aetiology, pathogenesis, intervention and cure—rather than, as has commonly been the case, leaving such questions largely to the domains of the life sciences and biomedicine?"[5]

In a similar vein, Whitehead and Woods open the *Edinburgh Handbook to the Critical Medical Humanities* by taking the "primal scene" for the medical humanities—the clinical encounter between doctor and patient that unfolds in the diagnosis of cancer—and asking "why this scene has come to matter so much in and to the field, what interests might be invested within it, and what is potentially occluded from view?"[6] At the same time as the medical humanities, more generally, has begun to invite a more critical stance, work in the literary medical humanities, specifically on illness narratives, has appeared to go in the opposite direction. While critics like Ann Jurecic and Stella Bolaki have done much "to counter dismissive views of illness memoirs as 'victim art'" (Bolaki), or "misery memoirs" (Jurecic), on first glance it appears to have come at the cost of their criticality.[7] By embracing models of reading practice informed more by Eve Kosofsky Sedgwick's "reparative reading" than Paul Ricoeur's "hermeneutics of suspicion," Jurecic and Bolaki seem to turn away from calls to make the medical humanities "critical."[8] *Pace* this "postcritical" reductive response to Jurecic and Bolaki, their work demands new forms of critical engagement. "What options," Jurecic asks, "are there other than didactic humanism of those who see narrative as redemptive or the radical doubt promoted by contemporary cultural and literary criticism?"[9] Similarly, Bolaki finds in "formal complexity, ambiguity and open-endedness ... important tools for challenging instrumental approaches to the medical humanities."[10] Both Jurecic and Bolaki find justification for this new criticality as a nuanced response to the emergence of illness narratives, a genre that is self-evidently oriented towards the medical humanities. As such, they are understandably interested in condition: they are, of course, concerned with somatic awareness, but most specifically as it relates to illness.

In an effort "to extend the gaze of medical humanities from the clinical interaction to critically examin[e] the evidence base that underlies that interaction," Jane Macnaughton and Havi Carel aim "to apply medical humanities understanding and approaches to the study of 'somatic' phenomena—breathing and breathlessness—with a view to challenging and broadening the evidence base on which breathing symptomatology is addressed clinically."[11] What Macnaughton and Carel propose, then, is to turn our attention from illness, broadly conceived, to its constitutive parts or symptoms, like breathlessness. They argue that "breathing and breathlessness [are] phenomena pregnant with historical, cultural and existential meanings that are often overlooked in the clinical context."[12]

This oversight constitutes an epistemic gap: "an apparently unbridgeable mismatch of understanding not only of knowledge but also of how that knowledge might be obtained, between the clinic and the person who experiences breathlessness."[13]

Such a gap can only be bridged by interdisciplinary approaches. Carel, for instance, shows how the experience of breathlessness, in an expanded, phenomenological sense should include a geography, an epistemic framework and a social architecture.[14] Breathlessness frames perceptions about the climate and the built environment. These become more or less hostile to the person with breathlessness. At the same time, the immediacy of the experience of breathlessness creates an epistemic mismatch between the person suffering and the person observing: the experience is all-consuming for the sufferer, while remaining all too invisible to the observer. Both Macnaughton and Carel argue that cultural responses to breath have an important constituting role to play in this philosophical and medical humanities work. But, while some of this cultural critique has developed in response to film, most responses to breath in literature are isolated to their particular area of literary studies.[15] This book proposes to address this inattention to breath, by considering how breath works in literature. In this sense, it prepares the ground for further conversations on the role its insights might play in developing an applied literary intervention on conversations about breath in the medical humanities.

In developing our reading of breath within the literary medical humanities, then, it might seem natural that we, too, should aim to address the breath–illness relation. Were we to focus on this relation, we might attend more closely to our second example above, Michael Symmons Roberts's *Breath*, which also appears in Macnaughton and Carel's work. But two interventions in the health psychology of breathlessness, both led by Ad A. Kaptein, warn us off moving too quickly from literary breathlessness to illness proper.[16] Kaptein et al. argue that literary texts, when read alongside cases of respiratory illness, may be put to a variety of "uses," whether educational, empathy raising or behaviour-changing.[17] Additionally, "an important aspect of this documentation is the view that the representation in novels, poems, films, music, and paintings of various respiratory illnesses reflects how patients experience their respiratory disease."[18] By way of example, the authors take Raymond Queneau's "descriptions of an episode of severe acute asthma" in *The Skin of Dreams* and suggest that "reading the quotation aloud will induce breathlessness in the listener."[19] Reading the quotation, aloud or otherwise, may attend to certain features of the "sensation" of breathless, but it is unlikely to precipitate the kind of empathetic response anticipated by Kaptein et al.:

> Louis with his two fists propped on his knees, Louis, bent over, begins to breathe badly … he is in the process of becoming conscious of his respiration. He cannot be said to be panting … but he is affected … afflicted with a constriction of the lungs, of pulmonary muscles, of the pulmonous nerves, of the pulmonic canals … it is kind of stifling … that starts from below, that also starts from both sides at once, it is a thoracic stifling, an encirclement of the respiratory barrel. And now something is very wrong. It is worse than strangling, worse than encirclement, an anatomical nightmare, a metaphysical anguish, a revolt …[20]

Kaptein et al. do not support their claim that reading this passage aloud will induce breathlessness with any evidence, whether from readers' report or the text itself. In its English translation, the passage appears to be more concerned with conveying breathlessness through repetition and qualification than mimetic stimulation. Alliteration ("begins to breathe badly"), emphasis ("Louis … Louis") and enumeration ("an anatomical nightmare, a metaphysical anguish, a revolt") cause the eye, or the ear, to tarry on certain details, while also attempting to revise or refine descriptions of these details ("affected … afflicted"; "that starts from below, that also starts from both sides at once"). Perhaps these tropes induce breathlessness; perhaps they do not. Certainly, they demonstrate "the process of becoming conscious" of something to do with respiration, even if it is not the direct, unmediated, mimetic "sensation" of it, envisaged by Kaptein et al. Indeed, the case studies that follow will consider how stylistic features, including but not limited to repetition and qualification, might develop a sense of how breathing and breathlessness comes to be mediated through literature.

There are, of course, examples of clinical writers who nuance literary representations of respiration. François-Bernard Michel's *Le Souffle coupé: Respirer et écrire* explores chronic breathlessness as a stylistic feature.[21] Michel's study of "breathless" French writers of the nineteenth and twentieth centuries builds a theory of breathless style around the asthma of Queneau, Marcel Proust and Prosper Mérimée, the coughing of Paul Valéry, and the tuberculosis of Jules Laforgue, André Gide and Albert Camus. In this sense, he performs that "physiology of style" that Walter Benjamin would identify, but not explore, in Proust's syntax: "Proust's syntax rhythmically and step by step reproduces his fear of suffocating. And his ironic, philosophical, didactic reflections invariably are the deep breath with which he shakes off the weight of memories."[22] Michel, Professor of Respiratory Medicine in the Medical Faculty at Montpellier when his book was published, draws these moments of breath-inflected poetics together under the strange dialectic of the asthmatic. The asthmatic is not ill, except for those moments of crisis when she feels as if she will "die of suffocation."[23] Asthma, in Michel's reading, is marked, since it is only present, in a phenomenological sense, during a crisis; otherwise, it is absent, for all intents and purposes, a non-existent illness. For this reason, the reading of "asthmatic style" concerns itself primarily with "crisis": the moment the asthmatic "refuses to breathe out and, at the same time, refuses the essential reality of human biology, the natural rhythms of the body."[24]

All of this might simply affirm that breathlessness's immanence, its resistance to metaphor, recalls Susan Sontag's key insight in *Illness and its Metaphors*, that "illness is *not* a metaphor and that the most truthful way of regarding illness ... is one most purified of, most resistant to, metaphoric thinking."[25] When breath approaches the medical, in literary studies, its attention to medical issues either dissimulates any reliance on aesthetic mediation whatsoever, or, alternately, is engulfed by those metaphors of which Sontag remained so suspicious. These two tendencies, of great interest when dealing directly with breathing bodies, present difficulties for developing the role for literary mediation in the growing scholarship on breathing and breathlessness in medical humanities. Indeed, texts do not "represent" breathing bodies, nor do they, whatever the avowed intention, actually "mimic" a breathless syntax, however attractive that thought might be. A preferable position to take might follow Sasha Engelmann's work on air poetics, which "provokes thought toward the material, aesthetic and affective qualities of airy experiences."[26] Engelmann proposes an air poetics that "dissolves distinctions of body-environment boundaries, renders explicit air's materiality and fosters an openness to the affective intensity of air in shaping the patterns of atmospheric space-time."[27] A similarly attentive response to breath poetics attends to the breath's interactions across body-environment boundaries, disclosing the intensities, pleasures and pains of air's materiality, and questioning whether the affects produced are necessarily useful or desirable. By re-engaging aesthetic theories of breathlessness, and their origins in sensation, literary descriptions of breathing and breathlessness might, *pace* Sontag, be more interesting for their aesthetic processes than for any exacting mimetic accuracy.

This book offers itself as a set of literary responses to breath, not to close down conversations with the literary medical humanities, but precisely to expand its conceptual scope in responding to the long intellectual history to this vehicle of the soul. Whether the basis for cosmological metaphor (*pneuma*), the limit point of the rhetorical arts (*cola*), the object of medical scrutiny (*respiration*), or the principle of corporeal unity (*prana*), breath understood as metonym for life itself, rather than as a discrete physiological process, has often acted as a philosophical first principle.[28] To expand this sense of breath beyond the illness narrative, then, I want to consider some of the ways in which metonymic breath has also had its share of tensions.

After all, it is against breath as first principle that Jacques Derrida set his *Grammatology*, his famous response to the long tradition of "natural writing," which "is immediately united to the voice and to breath."[29] Such writing, Derrida argues, "is not grammatological but pneumatological."[30] In Michael Naas's gloss,

> Grammatology would in effect announce the end or the closure of a certain Greco-Christian pneumatology, that is, the closure of an epoch where what is privileged is language's seemingly natural relationship to speech, voice, the verb, the living breath and so on, as opposed to writing.[31]

If anything, the weight of aesthetic theory on the breath in literature appears to work against this closure. Breath still enjoys a privileged place in aesthetic theories of composition and meaning-making, linguistic or otherwise. Whether as measure or as rest, breath confers metre, dictates pauses, conditions meaning or points to the limits of semantics. It presences the actor, musician, artist to a particular moment in a particular place. In its absence, it still seems to regulate, to pattern, the written word, through diacritics, notation or typographical spacing. Breath is foundational.

Since poetry, in the vitalist tradition, has often aspired to recreate elements of the spoken word, poets have received a disproportionately high attention. Much of this work, in Anglophone poetry, has focused on poets with a biographical connection to breathlessness, like John Keats, or on poets whose works challenge "normal breathing," through the length of the line (Walt Whitman) or the use of sprung rhythm (Gerard Manley Hopkins), or on poets whose manifestos attempt to recharge writing with etiolated vitalism (Charles Olson, or Allen Ginsberg, or Jack Kerouac).[32] In the German tradition, Rainer Maria Rilke and Paul Celan represent rich sources of "breath-thought" and "breath writing."[33] German literature is also abundant in respirational prose: the walking texts of Robert Walser, the tuberculin fantasies of Thomas Mann and the suffocating rhythms of Thomas Bernhard.[34]

In performance studies, "breathwork" comprises a number of widely used and conceptually sophisticated techniques.[35] Sreenath Nair, for instance, has considered in great depth how Yogic medicine has been integrated into the performance practices of Kerala, particularly Kudivattam.[36] This is more an observation of localised universalism than orientalising exoticism, since similar insights have been made of the performance tradition that arises in response to Samuel Beckett's *Breath*.[37] Since performance avows, in some sense or another, a presence, studies of performance can make more assumptions about shared embodiment than is ever possible in the transmitted literary word.

The challenge, then, is to address the multivalent, contradictory meanings of breath in these different aesthetic contexts. Whether or not Derrida was successful in announcing "the closure" of "Greco-Christian pneumatology," his attempt to decentre breath affirms that an antimony exists: either language has a natural relationship to speech, thereby prioritising the breath for the language arts; or writing, as grammatology rather than pneumatology, precedes, and thereby sets itself in contrast to, the breath. Bearing this very antimony in mind, literary investigations may focus on the intersections of both poles and ask how characteristics of "writing" pervade spoken breath-rhythms and how breath inscribes itself in writing.

In the essays that follow, the authors stage a series of aesthetic interventions into the ways this travel happens. Breath functions differently in literature from the medieval period to the present. These essays do not presume to trace a complete intellectual history of breath, even in the Anglophone tradition to which they restrict themselves. Nor do they claim to present a comprehensive understanding of breath in Anglophone literature. Rather, they propose, through a series of case examples, techniques by which "breath" might be more rigorously thought as useful, if under-examined, resource for thinking about literature. In keeping with the nature of the intervention, the essays insert themselves at interstices between common assumptions about breath and ways these assumptions are taken up or rejected in literary texts.

Consider, for instance, Charles Olson's poetic manifesto, "Projective Verse," perhaps the most influential Anglophone text about respiratory poetics to be written in the mid-twentieth century.[38] "Projective Verse" tracks the antimony between natural language and grammatology precisely in its celebration of breath as both foundation of natural language and feature of language's work in the age of technical reproduction. It balances a celebration of the poet's breath against an anti-vitalist coding of breath to the spacings of the typewriter. So, it begins: "Verse now, 1950, if it is to go ahead, if it is to be of essential use, must, I take it, catch up and put into itself certain laws and possibilities of the breath, of the breathing of the man who writes as well as of his listenings."[39]

This vitalism, however, is muted by the typewriter: "It is the advantage of the typewriter that, due to its rigidity and its space precisions, it can, for a poet, indicate exactly the breath, the pauses, the suspensions even of syllables, the juxtapositions even of parts of phrases, which he intends."[40] To be sure, Olson's "intentions" do maintain the pneumatological primacy of speech, criticised by Derrida. Breath, as a pneumatic essence, still underwrites the typewriter. But, implicit in Olson's account, is the idea that writing, or its presentation on the page, can dictate the patterns of breath, rather than, as seems in a natural writing, the other way round. Typography marks the breath in a way that differs significantly to rhyme, rhythm or even diacritics.[41]

Perhaps because breath functions so easily as an aesthetic substrate, it has been difficult to say anything substantial about it, in itself.[42] So often the vehicle for metaphors, breath is remarkably resistant to explication as tenor. Less metaphor, then, than marker. Marking designates a word whose phonological, grammatical or semantic features distinguish it from its dominant, "default" meaning.[43] Marking, as concept, begins as linguistic deviation from the breath. Nikolai Trubetzkoy, the first theorist of linguistic markedness, introduces it in his foundational *Principles of Phonology*: "In any correlation based on the manner of overcoming an obstruction a 'natural' absence of marking is attributable to that opposition member whose production requires the least deviation from normal breathing. The opposing member is then of course the marked member."[44] By asserting the unmarked as "the least deviation from normal breath," Trubetzkoy elevates the breath to a vitalist absolute: a normative measure. Markedness may have originated in biological correspondence with normal breathing patterns, but, as it became embedded in linguistic discourses, across phonetics, morphology and functional grammar, it demanded a less vitalist, more contextual approach. Deviation later came to be measured not through "normality," but through consistencies or inconsistencies, in context.

Marking, as contextual deviation, has implications for how we understand breath, when it appears as a signifier. Since novels, plays, poems or short stories have no need to mention the breath, of characters, speakers, or as metaphoric constructions, any mention of breath necessarily contributes either to a narrative message or the concerns of its method.[45] Breath contributes to the narrative or the description, but it functions as neither a narrative device, nor a descriptive detour. This link between world and subjective experience has important consequences for thinking subject–space relations. Not being necessary or optimal for concision or meaning, a "superfluous" mention of breath must therefore designate an emphasis. This assertion relies on a structuralist understanding of breath: it may be taken as an arbitrary sign, whose referent is marked by virtue of unusual semantic or syntactic activity. Again, we find a movement of concepts, whereby breath travels between vitalism and machinism.

Our essays draw out the possible ways in which marked breath may indeed be explicated, whether in its relation to affective trauma, to Galenic humours, to embodied aesthetic theory, to rhetorical poetics or to political metaphors. Deliberately drawing attention to aspects beyond representation and mimesis, they explore breath and breathlessness across various literary genres and in different historical and cultural areas. Beginning with the medieval period, Corinne Saunders considers the critical role breath plays in reflecting affective experience in Chaucer's romances. In his treatment of affect, Chaucer draws on medical theories of the time to portray how the movements of the vital spirit create powerful physical responses, which at their most extreme cause swooning and breathlessness. This physiological emphasis, central to Chaucer's depiction of love and grief, and his treatment of gender, infuses his use of romance conventions with originality. Moving forward in time to the early modern period, Naya Tsentourou addresses a historical episteme in which the sigh comes to signify wasted energy, with particular implications for the staging and direction of Shakespeare's *Hamlet*. The essay traces the slippery significations of sighing: hypocritical, instrumental, communicative, self-consuming and self-revealing, breathing in *Hamlet* has no fixed referent but shifts as often as the characters shift their position and perspective, constantly pointing to the impossibility of ordering an individual's or even a state's disordered breathing pattern. Peter Garratt's contribution is dedicated to the impact respiration—as metaphor, physiological process and embodied response—had on Victorian aesthetics. Late nineteenth-century attempts to define aesthetic experience in terms of its attendant physiological reactions still drew on breath's immaterial poetic associations (air, wind, spirit) while being alert to the way respiratory control shifts easily between voluntary and involuntary modes of experience (will/automation). Stefanie Heine explores how in post-war America the Beat writers configured a body-based poetics around breath that parallels concerns with orality and breathing in Ancient Rhetoric. Tracing these parallels shows how the supposedly new American poetry is in fact a Renaissance of classical thought and the idea of a pure bodily writing evoked by Allen Ginsberg and Jack Kerouac is upset by the cultural memory invoked. Finally, Arthur Rose addresses how breath becomes a sociopolitical concern in postcolonial literature, focusing particularly on Salman Rushdie. Considering the relation between breathing bodies and contested environments in *The Moor's Last Sigh*, the essay investigates how a combat breathing in Franz Fanon's sense links the postcolonial subject to their condition of being-in-the-world.

In its earliest iterations, this book's working title was *Breathroutes: Interventions into Respiratory Writing*. With the implicit reference to Celan, we want to provoke our readers into thinking of "breath" as more than simply a physiological signifier that maps onto an aesthetic preoccupation. We hope our essays track those moments when texts turn towards their own relationship with breath, to think through breath. In this way, we follow Jean-Thomas Tremblay, who concludes his introduction to a recent special issue with the poignant phrase: "no one is ever just breathing."[46] At the same time, we offer these essays as avenues for opening up, rather than closing down, further efforts to read breath in literature.

Notes

1. Irigaray (2004, 165). See also Škof and Holmes (2013) and Škof and Berndtson (2018).
2. Hulme (1988, 216).
3. Symmons Roberts (2008, 103–104).
4. See, for instance, Hawkins (1993), Frank (1995) and Charon (2006).
5. Viney et al. (2015, 3).
6. Whitehead and Woods (2016, 2).
7. Jurecic (2012, 22) and Bolaki (2016, 10).
8. Sedgwick (2003) and Ricoeur (1974). See also Felski (2011).
9. Jurecic (2012, 26).
10. Bolaki (2016, 16).
11. Macnaughton and Carel (2016, 294).
12. Ibid., 295.
13. Ibid.
14. Carel (2016, 106–129).
15. For responses to breath in film, see Quinlivan (2011), and special issues by Garwood and Greene (2016), and Tremblay (2018). Further references to breath in literature in the chapters that follow.
16. Kaptein and Lyons (2009) and Kaptein et al. (2015).
17. Kaptein et al. (2015).
18. Ibid., 252.
19. Kaptein et al. (2015, 249–250).
20. Queneau (1987, 11–12).
21. Michel (1984).
22. Benjamin (1968, 214).
23. Michel (1984, 7).
24. Ibid., 195.
25. Sontag (1978, 3).
26. Engelmann (2015).
27. Engelmann (2015, 432). See also Ash (2013).
28. On *pneuma*, see Horky (2018); on *cola* and the Buber-Rosenzweig bible, see Friedman (1988, 61); on *respiration*, see Culotta (1972); on *prana*, see Sivananda (1935).
29. Derrida (1997, 17).
30. Ibid.
31. Naas (2011, 30).
32. On Keats (and Coleridge), see O'Gorman (2011) and Kay (2016), and on breath in Romanticism, see Abrams (1957); on Whitman, see Ginsberg's "Improvisation in Beijing" (Ginsberg 1994); on Hopkins, see Dau (2005).

33. Rilke (1923), Celan (2011).
34. Walser (1917), Mann (1924), Bernhard (1981).
35. See, for example, Berry (1973) and Boston and Cook (2009).
36. Nair (2007).
37. See Goudouna (2018).
38. Olson (1966).
39. Ibid., 15.
40. Ibid., 22.
41. For the epistemic shift brought about by the typewriter, see Kittler (1999).
42. See, in a parallel argument, Macnaughton (2018).
43. Markedness has a fraught history in linguistics, primarily because it is difficult to assert unequivocally whether a particular inflection, form or meaning of a word is unmarked (dominant), or marked (subordinate). Although I will return to markedness's verifiability, for the moment I want to consider its usefulness in denoting the multiple ways that an author might place a stress on a word, phrase or syntactic form.
44. Trubetzkoy (1969, 146).
45. At the same time, if certain works are obviously "about" breath and therefore mark it for thematic and structural purposes, it does not follow that other novels, which do not take breath as an obvious thematic or structural concern, have unmarked breath. Indeed, of all the modal elaborations available to the novelist, realist or other, the least necessary has to be the mention of breath. Since no character in a novel need breathe, or, at least, no mention is necessary, all references to breath are significant and may be taken as marked to some extent or another by virtue of an emphasis principle. For a similar argument on the stylistic significance of "heavy breathing" and *respiración pesada* in English, Russian and Spanish literature (and translation), see Chapter 10 of Magrinyà (2015).
46. Tremblay (2018, 96).

References

Abrams, M.H. 1957. The Correspondent Breeze: A Romantic Metaphor. *The Kenyon Review* 19 (1): 113–114.

Ash, James. 2013. Rethinking Affective Atmospheres: Technology, Perturbation and Space Times of the Non-human. *Geoforum* 49: 20–28.

Benjamin, Walter. 1968. The Image of Proust. In *Illuminations*, trans. Harry Zohn, intro. Hannah Arendt, 201–215. New York: Schocken Books.

Bernhard, Thomas. 1981. *Der Atem: Eine Entscheidung*. München: Deutscher Taschenbuch Verlag.

Berry, Cicely. 1973. *Voice and the Actor*. London: Wiley Blackwell.

Bolaki, Stella. 2016. *Illness as Many Narratives: Arts, Medicine and Culture*. Edinburgh: Edinburgh University Press.
Boston, Jane, and Rena Cook (eds.). 2009. *Breath in Action: The Art of Breath in Vocal and Holistic Practice*. London: Jessica Kingsley.
Carel, Havi. 2016. *Phenomenology of Illness*. Oxford: Oxford University Press.
Celan, Paul. 2011. *The Meridian: Final Version—Drafts—Materials*, ed. Bernhard Böschenstein and Heino Schmull, trans. Pierre Joris. Stanford: Stanford University Press.
Charon, Rita. 2006. *Narrative Medicine: Honoring the Stories of Illness*. New York: Oxford University Press.
Culotta, Charles A. 1972. *Respiration and the Lavoisier Tradition: Theory and Modification, 1777–1850*. Philadelphia: Transactions of the American Philosophical Society.
Dau, Duo. 2005. The Caress of God's Breath in Gerard Manley Hopkins. *Sydney Studies in English* 31: 39–60.
Derrida, Jacques. 1997. *Of Grammatology*, trans. Gayatri Chakravorty Spivak. Baltimore: Johns Hopkins University Press.
Engelmann, Sasha. 2015. Toward a Poetics of Air: Sequencing and Surfacing Breath. *Transactions of the Institute of British Geographers* 30 (3): 430–444.
Felski, Rita. 2011. Critique and the Hermeneutics of Suspicion. *M/C Journal* 15 (1). http://journal.media-culture.org.au/index.php/mcjournal/article/view/431. Accessed 3 May 2018.
Frank, Arthur. 1995. *The Wounded Storyteller: Body, Illness and Ethics*. Chicago: University of Chicago Press.
Friedman, Maurice S. 1988. *Martin Buber's Life and Work*. Detroit: Wayne State University Press.
Garwood, Ian, and Liz Greene. 2016. Breath and the Body of the Voice in Cinema. *Music, Sound and the Moving Image* 10 (2): 105–107.
Ginsberg, Allen. 1994. Improvisation in Beijing. In *Cosmopolitan Greetings: Poems, 1986–1992*. New York: HarperCollins.
Goudouna, Sozita. 2018. *Beckett's Breath: Antitheatricality and the Visual Arts*. Edinburgh: Edinburgh University Press.
Hawkins, Anne Hunsaker. 1993. *Reconstructing Illness: Studies in Pathography*. West Lafayette: Purdue University Press.
Horky, Phillip (ed.). 2018. *Cosmos in the Ancient World*. Cambridge: Cambridge University Press.
Hulme, Keri. 1988. *Te Kaihau/The Windeater*. London: Sceptre.
Irigaray, Luce. 2004. The Age of Breath. In *Luce Irigaray: Key Writings*, 165–170. London: Continuum.
Jurecic, Ann. 2012. *Illness as Narrative*. Pittsburgh: University of Pittsburgh Press.

Kaptein, Ad A., and Antonia C. Lyons. 2009. The Doctor, the Breath and Thomas Bernhard: Using Novels in Health Psychology. *Journal of Health Psychology* 14 (2): 161–170.

Kaptein, Ad A., Frans Meulenberg, and Joshua M. Smyth. 2015. A Breath of Fresh Air: Images of Respiratory Illness in Novels, Poems, Films, Music, and Paintings. *Journal of Health Psychology* 20 (3): 246–258.

Kay, Andrew. 2016. Conspiring with Keats: Towards a Poetics of Breathing. *European Romantic Review* 27 (5): 563–581.

Kittler, Friedrich A. 1999. *Gramophone, Film, Typewriter*, trans. Geoffrey Winthrop-Young and Michael Wurtz. Stanford: Stanford University Press.

Macnaughton, Jane. 2018. Making Breath Visible. Working Paper.

Macnaughton, Jane, and Havi Carel. 2016. Breathing and Breathlessness in Clinic and Culture: Using Critical Medical Humanities to Bridge an Epistemic Gap. In *The Edinburgh Companion to the Critical Medical Humanities*, ed. Anne Whitehead et al., 294–309. Edinburgh: Edinburgh University Press.

Magrinyà, Luis. 2015. *Estilo Rico, Estilo Pobre: Guía Práctica Para Expresarse y Escribirse*. Barcelona: Penguin Random House.

Mann, Thomas. 1924. *Der Zauberberg*. Berlin: S. Fischer Verlag.

Michel, François-Bernard. 1984. *Le Souffle coupé: Respirer et écrire*. Paris: Gallimard.

Naas, Michael. 2011. Pneumatology, Pneuma, Souffle, Breath. In *Reading Derrida's of Grammatology*, ed. Sean Gaston and Ian Maclachan, 28–31. London: Continuum.

Nair, Sreenath. 2007. *Restoration of Breath: Consciousness and Performance*. Amsterdam: Rodopi.

O'Gorman, Frances. 2011. Coleridge, Keats, and the Science of Breathing. *Essays in Criticism* 61 (4): 365–381.

Olson, Charles. 1966. Projective Verse. In *Selected Writings*, ed. Robert Creeley, 15–26. New York: New Directions.

Queneau, Raymond. 1987. *The Skin of Dreams*, trans. H.J. Kaplan. London: Atlas Press.

Quinlivan, Davina. 2011. *The Place of Breath in Cinema*. Edinburgh: Edinburgh University Press.

Ricoeur, Paul. 1974. *The Conflict of Interpretations: Essays in Hermeneutics*, ed. Don Ihde. Evanston: Northwestern University Press.

Rilke, Rainer Maria. 1923. *Die Sonette an Orpheus*. Leipzig: Insel Verlag.

Sedgwick, Eve Kosofsky. 2003. *Touching Feeling: Affect, Pedagogy, Performativity*. Durham: Duke University Press.

Sivananda, Sri Swami. 1935. *The Science of Pranayama*. Rishikesh, Uttar Pradesh: The Divine Life Society.

Škof, Lenart, and Emily A. Holmes (eds.). 2013. *Breathing with Luce Irigaray*. London: Bloomsbury.
Škof, Lenart, and Petri Berndtson (eds.). 2018. *Atmospheres of Breathing*. Albany: SUNY Press.
Sontag, Susan. 1978. *Illness as Metaphor*. New York: Farrar, Straus & Giroux.
Symmons Roberts, Michael. 2008. *Breath*. London: Vintage Books.
Tremblay, Jean-Thomas. 2018. Breath: Image and Sound, an Introduction. *New Review of Film and Television Studies* 16 (2): 93–97.
Trubetzkoy, N.S. 1969. *Principles of Phonology*, trans. Christiane A.M. Baltaxe. Berkeley: University of California Press.
Viney, William, Felicity Callard, and Angela Woods. 2015. Critical Medical Humanities: Embracing Entanglement, Taking Risks. *Medical Humanities* 41: 2–7.
Walser, Robert. 1917. *Der Spaziergang*. Frauenfeld: Huber.
Whitehead, Anne, and Angela Woods. 2016. Introduction. In *The Edinburgh Companion to the Critical Medical Humanities*, ed. Anne Whitehead et al., 1–31. Edinburgh: Edinburgh University Press.

Open Access This chapter is licensed under the terms of the Creative Commons Attribution 4.0 International License (http://creativecommons.org/licenses/by/4.0/), which permits use, sharing, adaptation, distribution and reproduction in any medium or format, as long as you give appropriate credit to the original author(s) and the source, provide a link to the Creative Commons license and indicate if changes were made.

The images or other third party material in this chapter are included in the chapter's Creative Commons license, unless indicated otherwise in a credit line to the material. If material is not included in the chapter's Creative Commons license and your intended use is not permitted by statutory regulation or exceeds the permitted use, you will need to obtain permission directly from the copyright holder.

CHAPTER 2

The Play of Breath: Chaucer's Narratives of Feeling

Corinne Saunders

Abstract This essay explores the treatment of breath and breathlessness in the imaginative fiction of Geoffrey Chaucer. Chaucer draws on medieval medical theories, rooted in classical thought, to portray the ways that motions of the vital spirit—closely connected with breath—create powerful physical responses, which at their most extreme cause sighs and swoons. According to this pre-Cartesian world view, mind, body and affect are intimately connected. The movement of breath plays a key role in Chaucer's depiction of the experiences of emotion, particularly love and grief, and in his treatment of gender. This physiological emphasis creates narratives of feeling that are deeply embodied. The essay focuses on Chaucer's romance writing, in particular, *The Book of the Duchess*, *Troilus and Criseyde* and *The Legend of Good Women*.

Keywords Breath · Swoon · Sigh · Vital spirits · Affect · Emotion · Body

> I am as confident as I am of anything that, in myself, the stream of thinking (which I recognize emphatically as a phenomenon) is only a careless name for what, when scrutinized, reveals itself to consist chiefly of the stream of my breathing. (William James, "Does Consciousness Exist?")[1]

For William James, breath, "ever the original of spirit", is "the essence out of which philosophers have constructed the entity known to them as consciousness."[2] The coincidence of breath with embodied experience, thought, feeling and consciousness is nowhere more evident than in medieval writing. Breath is a flashpoint, a culturally complex term linked both to ideas of health and life and to their converse, illness and death. It is also essential to medieval physiological models where mind, body and affect are understood to be profoundly connected. While the conventions of extreme emotion typical of medieval romance writing seem far distant from reality, the world of lovesickness, swoons and sighs taps into medieval understandings of breathing, feeling and being in the world in ways that are surprisingly realist.[3] Breathing and consciousness are inextricable, and breathlessness is directly connected with disruptions of thought and feeling.

Medieval medical theory depended on the humoural theory developed by the Greek physician Hippocrates (c. 460–c. 370 BC) and refined by Galen (129–c. 216 AD): both physical and mental health required the balance of the four humours, and medieval medicine was oriented towards restoring this balance.[4] In contrast to post-Cartesian mind-body dualism, humoural theory necessitated the idea of a mind-body continuum. Ideas of mind and body were complicated by shifting theories of the soul, mental faculties and emotions. For Aristotle, while rational, intellective being was a quality of the soul, senses and cognitive faculties were situated in the heart; the idea of the heart as site of both understanding and feeling persisted in popular and literary culture through the Renaissance and beyond. According to this model, breathing was understood to be governed by the heart, the source of heat that caused the blood to pulse and flow and dilated the lungs, which drew in air; breath performed the essential role of cooling the heart through the bellows-like action of the lungs. Alexandrian medicine complicated Aristotle's theories both through a new emphasis on the brain as cognitive and sensory centre, and through theories of the "spirits" elaborated by Galen, which were central to Arabic medicine and dominated medical thought across the Middle Ages. According to Galen's theory, "*pneuma* (air), the life breath of the cosmos," was drawn into the body and transformed within the three primary organs into three kinds.[5] The "natural spirits" created in the liver were carried through the veins and governed generation, growth, nutrition and digestion. The "vital spirits" created in the heart through the mixture of air and blood were carried through the arteries and heated and animated the body, governing breathing. These vital spirits were transformed in the brain into "animal spirits," carried through the nerves and controlling sensation, movement and thought, fuelling the workings of the brain.[6] The lungs continued to play a central role in this model: as well as cooling the heart they provided the air that would be transformed, mixed with blood, to the vital spirits. The classical model of the lungs is explicated by Isidore of Seville (c. 560–636) in his influential *Etymologies*: "pulmo," the lung, is so named in Greek

> because it is a fan (*flabellum*) for the heart, in which the *pneuma*, that is, the breath, resides, through which the lungs are both put in motion and kept in motion – from this also the lungs are so named. ... The lungs are the engine of the body.[7]

Isidore's *Etymologies*, widely circulated throughout the Middle Ages, contributed to the stability of classical models.

The twelfth century saw a "Renaissance" of learning, the result of the *translatio studii*, the movement of texts from East to West, partly through access to classical and Arabic works brought by the Muslim expansion into Europe. Galenic physiology was disseminated to the Christian West via Latin translations of Arabic and Greek medical texts in the early twelfth century, in particular the works of Constantine of Africa (d. before 1098/99). Constantine's *Pantegni theorica*, which translated parts of the tenth-century Arabic medical encyclopaedia of "Haly Abbas" (Ali ibn al-'Abbas al-Majusi), itself based on Galenic works, along with a translation of the treatise on the Galenic theory of humours and spirits by the ninth-century scholar and physician "Johannitius" (Hunayn ibn Ishaq), *Isagoge Johanitii in Tegni Galeni*, became foundation texts for the *Articella* or *Ars medicine*, the collection of six medical works which formed the basis of Western medical theory and entered the university curriculum in the thirteenth century.[8] The medical theorist Bartholomaeus Anglicus, whose *De proprietatibus rerum* (*On the Properties of Things*, c. 1240) was translated into English by the natural philosopher John of Trevisa (c. 1399), elaborates in detail the theory of the spirits, drawing directly on Constantine. He sets out the processes of breathing and the workings of the vital spirits or "virtue of life" with careful attention to physiology:

> Aftir þe vertu of kynde folewiþ þe vertu of lif þat 3eueþ lif to þe body and haþ place in þe herte. Out of þe herte comeþ lif to al þe limes. ... Þis vertu of lif openiþ þe herte by worchinge of þe longen and draweþ in aier to the hert and sendiþ forþ from þe herte to oþir limes by smale weyes. And by help of þe vertu þat closith and riueþ [pierces] and openith þe herte þis vertu worchiþ and makeþ breþinge in a beest. And by breþinge þe brest meueþ continualliche, but sinewis and brawnes beþ first imeued. Þis blast, breþ, and onde [breath/spirit] is nedeful to slake þe kindeliche hete, and to foode of þe spirit of lif, and also to þe gendringe of þe spirit þat hatte *animalis* þat 3eueþ felinge and meuynge. Þe kepinge of þe kinde hete is a temperat indrawinge of coold aier and þe kepinge of þe spirit þat hatte *spiritus vitalis* "of lif". Of þe temperament of þis spirit is þe spirit gendrid þat hatte *animalis* þat 3eueþ felinge. Þerfore noþing is more nedeful to kepe and to saue þe lif þan breþ, wel disposid and ordeyned in alle pointis. All þis seiþ Constantinus in *Pantegni*.[9]

The role of breath is twofold: it cools the heart and generates the vital spirits, which are required to create the animal spirits. The model clearly signals the interdependence of mind and body, all fuelled by the breath.

It is easy to see how readily classical concepts of the *pneuma*, the life breath of the cosmos, transferred to Christian conceptions of the Holy Spirit, and to the Hebrew notion of *ruach*, the breath of God. The concept of *pneuma* is repeatedly employed in the New Testament, in particular by St. Paul, who takes up both classical and Old Testament notions. The Spirit of divinity and life is external to the individual, moving within the cosmos; but it is also inspiring and inspired, moving the souls of men and breathing new life—the life of the Spirit—into them. Christian conceptions of the soul, however, required distinctions between air and soul not made in classical theories of *pneuma* as world soul. Isidore of Seville is emphatic concerning the difference between soul—*anima, spiritus*—from the air breathed in through the mouth:

> ... we seem to stay alive by drawing air into the mouth. But this is quite clearly untrue, since the soul is generated much earlier than air can be taken into the mouth, because it is already alive in the mother's womb.[10]

Different theories competed across the Middle Ages. The *pneuma* was most typically viewed within a physiological framework as "the instrument of the soul" but could, in its "animal" form in the brain, also be understood as the corporeal aspect of a tripartite soul.[11] There is always some slippage between the idea of *pneuma*—the breath of God breathing life into man—and *pneuma/spiritus*, the breath. The concept of the "vital spirits" inevitably overlaps with that of the Holy Spirit, giving breath a special status as the animating force. Spirits are often written in the singular, heightening the overlap. The heat associated with the heart also created a physiological context for the prevalent imagery of fire frequently associated with the Holy Spirit, which descends in tongues of fire at Pentecost. Richard Rolle, for example, takes up this idea in his *Incendium Amoris* (*The Fire of Love*): the work opens with Rolle's memorable description of the physical sensation of the flame of divine love, so strong that he touches his breast to see whether his heart is literally on fire: "I cannot tell you how surprised I was the first time I felt my heart begin to warm. It was real warmth too, not imaginary, and it felt as if it were actually on fire."[12] The divine *pneuma* is understood as both air and fire, corresponding readily to physiological concepts of *pneuma* as breath and the vital spark of life.

The play of breath in all these senses underpins medieval theories of the emotions, to which the concept of the mind-body continuum was also essential. Such ideas resonate strikingly with the view of William James, radically anti-Cartesian in its time, of emotion as rooted in affect ("*the feeling of the same changes as they occur IS the emotion*,") with Merleau-Ponty's conception of embodiment, and with neuroscientific theories of affect and the role of emotion in cognition such as those of Antonio Damasio.[13] Medieval models understood emotions to occur through the movements of the vital spirits and natural heat produced in the heart and travelling through the arteries. They could be caused by direct sensory experience or by imagination and memory, but always had both physical and mental consequences. In extreme pleasure or anger, the vital spirits and accompanying heat moved out of the heart to other parts of the body: the heat might be visible in blushing, frenzy or manic movement. In extreme grief, distress or fear, or through a sudden shock, by contrast, the vital spirits and heat withdrew from the arteries into the heart. Such withdrawal of spirits was synonymous with withdrawal of breath and might cause unconsciousness or even death. Swoons, in particular, signal great grief, distress, terror or ecstasy. Sighs, intimately connected with emotional experience, also play a vital role as a means to purge and cool the overburdened or overheated heart. As Naya Tsentourou demonstrates in this volume in relation to *Hamlet*, sighs also came to be seen as dangerous: too many might cause the heart to dry out and wither. Etymology signals the close connection between sighs and swoons in the medieval period. The Middle English terms for sigh ("swough," also meaning a forceful motion or impetus, deriving from Old English "swōgan," to resound, sound, rush or roar) and swoon ("swoun," deriving from Old English "geswogen," in a faint/overcome, also ultimately from "-swōgan" ["āswōgan," to overcome]) are closely related, and may be spelt identically.[14] The sense of sudden motion and overwhelming force suggests the powerful affective movement of the spirits and its profound effects on body and breath.[15]

The writings of Geoffrey Chaucer engage in particularly striking detail with such conceptions of breath and vital spirits. Chaucer, like his contemporary John Gower, was both interested and well versed in natural philosophy and medicine. He was familiar with Bartholomaeus Anglicus' treatise, perhaps through John of Trevisa's translation, as well as with a range of other medical, philosophical and theological works. The play of breath in Chaucer's writing opens onto the exploration of mind, body and emotion, individual psychology and agency, and the power of affect. The interplay of thinking, feeling and breathing at moments of extreme emotion, positive and negative, is particularly revealing. Swoons and sighs are not simply conventional indicators of feeling but markers of profound, often formative affect that construct individual psychology. It is narratives that participate in the structures and emphases of romance, the imaginative fiction of the period, that engage most acutely with such emotional extremes, which are typically associated with the individual experience of love, its affects and its losses.

It is often an emphasis on the physicality of experience that takes Chaucer's depictions of emotion beyond convention. In Venus's temple in the *Parliament of Fowls*, the narrator sees painted on the walls stories of tragic love and hears the sound of "sykes [sighs] hoote as fyr"; "Whiche sikes were engendered with desyr, / That maden every auter for to brenne / Of newe flaume..."[16]: they are all caused by jealousy. Similarly, in the *Knight's Tale*, the walls of the Temple of Venus depict "[t]he broken slepes, and the sikes colde, / The sacred teeris and the waymentynge [lamenting], / The firy strokes of the desirynge" (1920– 22). Love is a highly physical phenomenon, a sickness. The topos finds its origins in classical poetry, particularly that of Ovid, but is much developed and heightened by medieval poets; medical writings of the period recognised lovesickness as a serious illness.[17] The thirteenth-century

Le Roman de la Rose begun by Guillaume de Lorris (c. 1237) and completed by Jean de Meun (c. 1275), and partly translated into English by Chaucer, offers the archetypal model of the lover wounded by the arrow shot by the God of Love.[18] With the shaft left in his heart, the narrator manifests the symptoms of lovesickness, changing colour, fainting and sighing in pain: "I anoon gan chaungen hewe / For grevaunce of my wounde newe, / That I agayn fell in swonyng / And sighede sore in compleynyng" (1865–68). The narrative of the *Roman de la Rose* suggests the physiology of the experience: the heart is literally wounded, and the effect of extreme affect on the vital spirits is manifest in the lover's loss of consciousness; his sighs breathe out the excessive heat of the spirits that overload the heart. The lover marvels to the God of Love at his own suffering, depicted with vivid physicality: "How ony man may lyve or laste / In such peyne and such brennyng, / In sorwe and thought and such sighing, / Ay unrelesed woo to make" (2726–29). Chaucer uses the idea to comic effect in his *Miller's Tale*, when the soon-to-be cuckolded husband John adopts the behaviour of a courtly lover in wooing his wife Alisoun, "[h]e siketh with ful many a sory swogh" (3619); the clerk Absolon follows suit. Proto-courtly behaviour and refined emotion contrast humorously with the frank sexuality of the tale: the sufferings of lovers are swiftly replaced by fulfilment or bawdy denial of desire. Chaucer's romances, by contrast, probe through the play of breath the painful extremes of emotional experience, the ways in which such affect shapes the psyche, and hence, the embodied quality of being.

Chaucer's earliest narrative poem, the dream vision *The Book of the Duchess* (1369–72), explores in acutely physiological terms the experiences of grief and loss, and the profound affects on heart and mind.[19] Underlying its narrative is the event it in some sense commemorates, the death of John of Gaunt's wife Blanche, Duchess of Lancaster in 1368/69. The poem concerns both physical and metaphorical "hert-huntyng" (1313)—not only the hart hunted by the emperor Octavien in the narrator's dream, but also the grief-stricken hearts of the narrator, of the classical heroine Alcyone, whose story the narrator reads to combat his insomnia, and of the Man in Black, the dream-figure whose loss echoes and surpasses the narrator's own melancholy. The frame of the dream is coloured by repeated references to the movements of breath and vital spirits in and out of the heart. The melancholy humour is depicted in terms of physical cooling: the withdrawal of the vital spirits into the heart has "sleyn [the narrator's] spirit of quyknesse" (26)—a sickness from which only one physician, his lady, can heal him. The inset story describes Alcyone's distress at the news of her husband Ceyx's death, which causes a movement of the spirits so violent that she swoons through withdrawal of breath: she is "as cold as ston" (123). The cold, heavy dullness of grief is further mirrored in Alcyone's "dede slep" (127), the description of Ceyx's corpse, "pale and nothyng rody" (143), the sleep of the gods in their dark, infernal cave and even the "dedly slepynge soun [sound]" (162) of water in the underworld. Finally, the narrator, who seems half asleep, a "mased thyng" (12) engrossed in his fantasies, himself falls asleep. The clustering images of sleep, death, melancholy, sorrow, heaviness and bewilderment creates something of the muted, melancholy atmosphere of Keats's *Ode on Melancholy*, "For shade to shade will come too drowsily, / And drown the wakeful anguish of the soul."[20]

In the dream-narrative of the Man in Black's loss, Chaucer offers remarkable physiological detail, much developed from his sources. The great physicians of history are evoked: "[n]oght Ypocras ne Galyen [Hippocrates or Galen]" (572) can treat the knight's sorrowful heart. The heart is depicted as fainting in grief, causing the spirits to withdraw:

> His sorwful hert gan faste faynte
> And his spirites wexen* dede;   *became
> The blood was fled for pure drede
> Doun to his herte, to make hym warm –
> For wel hyt feled the herte had harm. (488–92)

As vital spirits and blood move into the heart, the "membre principal" (495) of the body, colour and life are withdrawn: "al / Hys hewe chaunge and wexe grene / And pale, for ther noo blood ys sene / In no maner lym [limb] of hys" (496–99). His sorrows "lay so colde upon hys herte" that he wonders how he can live, and the withdrawal of vital spirits in turn deprives his brain of animal spirits so that his thought too is "hevy" (508, 509). Chaucer takes up and much extends the description in Machaut's *Jugement dou Roy de Behaingne* (c. 1340), one of his sources for the poem, of its grieving lady's heavy heartache, pallour and pensiveness. The Man in Black becomes the epitome of grief: "y am sorwe, and sorwe ys y" (597). His black attire, abstraction and melancholy might seem to render him an antecedent of Hamlet, though the cause of his grief is very different. In the Man in Black's long lament and account of the loss of his lady, the imagery of heartsickness and death recurs, contrasting with remembered health and happiness in courtship and marriage. In his final revelation of his lady's death, the affects of the loss of vital spirits are figured at their most extreme: "he wax as ded as stoon" (1300). With this, the "hert-huntyng" and dream are at an end, but there is no consolation: rather, death is memorialised in the poem, as the frozen affects of grief become art. The swooning figure of the Man in Black is transformed into the memorial poem, a complement to the marble effigy of his dead duchess commissioned by John of Gaunt.

The extended epic romance that begins the *Canterbury Tales*, the *Knight's Tale* (1386–88), again takes up the conventions of lovesickness, infusing them with physiological realism. In his depiction of the affects of love on the minds and bodies of the two cousins, Palamon and Arcite, who on seeing the lady Emilye walking in a Maytime garden suddenly fall in love with her, Chaucer interweaves with contemporary medical theory the ancient neo-Platonic conception of love as striking through the eyes to wound the heart. Palamon looks at Emilye, "And therwithal he bleynte and cride, 'A!' / As though he stongen were unto the herte" (1078–79). The heart is directly affected: the withdrawal of the vital spirits—blood and breath—into the heart signalled through the pain and pallour. Arcite's feeling is articulated in similar terms of mortal illness and echoed in the sighs that breathe out his burden: he "is hurt as muche as he, or moore. / And with a sigh he seyde pitously, / 'The fresshe beautee sleeth me sodeynly / Of hire that rometh in the yonder place; / And but I have hir mercy and hir grace, / That I may seen hire atte leeste weye, / I nam but deed; there nis namoore to seye'" (1116–22). Jealousy only heightens the extreme affects of withdrawal of vital spirits, seizing Palamon "by the herte / So woodly [madly] that he lyk was to biholde [to look upon was like] / The boxtree or the asshen dede and colde" (1300–2). The depiction of the deathly affects of love combines convention and realism. Chaucer elaborates on Arcite's malady by placing it as both mental and physical, using contemporaneous theories of the brain:

> ... lene he wex* and drye as is a shaft;*   *he became lean *stick
> His eyen holwe* and grisly to biholde,   *sunken
> His hewe falow* and pale as asshen colde,   *sickly yellow
> ...
> So feble eek were his spiritz, and so lowe,
> And chaunged so, that no man koude knowe

> His speche nor his voys, though men it herde.
> And in his geere* for al the world he ferde* *demeanour *behaved
> Nat oonly lik the loveris maladye
> Of Hereos*, but rather lyk manye,* *love-sickness *mania
> Engenderd of humour malencolik
> Biforen, in his celle fantastik.* (1362–76) *imagination

The passage addresses the affects of love on the animal spirits, into which the vital spirits are transformed in the brain. Chaucer may have drawn on Bartholomaeus Anglicus's description of how the melancholy humour works on the "celle fantastik," the ventricle of the brain controlling the imagination, to impair judgement and reason.[21] Whereas in grief the Man in Black's vital spirits withdraw into the heart, in extreme desire heat from the heart, and the accompanying vital spirits, are drawn in by the overactive brain, making the eyes appear hollow and the face pale. The resulting excess of animal spirits causes Arcite's inner senses to return again and again to the image of his beloved, bodying it forth repeatedly in his mind's eye in a kind of "manye" (1374), mania or frenzy. Looking in a mirror, he realises the dramatic effect on his own appearance: "[he] saugh that chaunged was al his colour, / And saugh his visage al in another kynde" (1400–1); he is able to return to Athens without being recognised. The movement of breath is as essential to the extremes of desire as it is to those of grief, causing the movement of the vital spirits into the brain, and the frenzied work of the animal spirits into which they are transformed. In a different way, the normal workings of the vital spirits are impaired: as when they are withdrawn into the heart, their excessive movement into the brain destroys physical health, emaciating and weakening the body and removing its colour and animation. Physical and mental, body and brain, are intimately connected, necessitating an understanding of emotional experience as deeply embodied and situated in the play of breath.

The end of the tale returns more explicitly to the issue of the vital spirits and breath in Chaucer's remarkably extensive account of the injury sustained by Arcite when, having won Emilye's hand in the grand tournament orchestrated by Theseus, he is thrown from his horse at the command of the god Saturn. The detail is notable for its physiological realism: pierced by his saddle bow, Arcite's breast swells, causing increasing pain in his heart because the clotted blood cannot be expelled and "[c]orrupteth" (decays, 2746). The poisonous matter presses on and causes to swell "[t]he pipes [tubes] of his longes"; all the muscles in his breast are "shent [destroyed] with venym and corrupcioun [decayed matter]" (2752–54). The spirits are prevented from their natural work: the poison cannot be expelled by the "vertu expulsif, or animal, / Fro thilke vertu cleped natural" (2749–50). The expulsive or "offeputtinge" property ("vertu") is envisaged in medical theory as a function of the natural spirits originating in the liver, ridding the body of waste: "þat puttiþ of what is greuous and noȝt accordinge"; this function is governed by the animal spirit, which "meueþ alle þe limes."[22] Because Arcite's movement is inhibited, the expulsion of poison cannot happen, and at the same time, the vital spirits animating the body are prevented from moving out from the heart to the lungs and arteries, while breathing cannot serve its natural function of cooling the heart. As "vital strengthe" (2802) withdraws, the "coold of deeth" falls upon Arcite's body (2800), leaving only the rational soul. Here Chaucer turns to the ancient model of thought and feeling as situated within the heart to convey rational being: "Oonly the intellect, withouten moore, / That dwelled in his herte syk and soore, / Gan faillen whan the herte felte deeth. / Dusked [grew dark] his eyen two and failled breeth" (2803–6). Chaucer employs extensive medical detail to create a powerful impression of the effects of a wound that prevents natural functioning of the body, and hence, the gradual failure of the spirits and the dying out of the intellect itself. Breathing and the vital spirits animate body and mind, and the intimate, physical connections between heart, spirits, breath, intellect and soul are crucial to Chaucer's realisation of being in the world.

Chaucer's epic romance *Troilus and Criseyde* (c. 1382–85) explores the complex intersections of mind, body and affect at the greatest length, in the narrative of the sorrows of Troilus, first falling in love with and then betrayed by his lady Criseyde. The play of breath as the vital spirits move in and out of the heart marks the process of love on Troilus' body in his sighs, tears, swoons and finally, his wasting away on grief. Love is painful and invasive, a punishment inflicted by the God of Love on Troilus for his laughter at the folly of lovers, and an affliction of both body and mind. Like *The Knight's Tale*, the narrative relies on the neo-Platonic concept of the connection between eyes and heart, but is also informed by detailed physiological theory. As Troilus's gaze rests on Criseyde, he is "astoned," a verb suggesting the withdrawal of vital spirits into the heart, which is caused to "sprede and rise" as if on fire, so that he "softe sighed" (I, 274, 278–89). The response is both conventional and medically alert: sighs are an instinctive response to the overheated heart. The gaze quickens desire, "affeccioun" (I, 296), a term that signals the physicality of feeling, its embeddedness in the movement of the vital spirits, which are drawn out of the heart to engage the passions, felt at once in body and in mind. The account of Troilus's feeling emphasises this extreme movement: "sodeynly hym thoughte he felte dyen, / Right with hire look, the spirit in his herte" (I, 306–7). His response is sighs and groans, which release the heart (I, 360). Chaucer repeatedly employs the imagery of burning, "hote fir" (I, 445, 490), evoking the heart's overheated quality as well as conventionally signalling desire. The work is suffused with imagery of heartsickness, which afflicts the body to the extent of causing Troilus to swoon, losing breath altogether: "[Troilus] no word seyde, / But longe he ley as stylle as he ded were; / And after this with sikynge he abreyde [started up]" (I, 722–24); again, sighing functions to relieve the heart. While Pandarus speaks, Troilus seems "in frenesie" (I, 727), a term used here to suggest not frenzy of movement but abstraction bordering on unconsciousness. Later, seeing Criseyde weep, Troilus feels "[t]he crampe of deth to streyne [constrain] hym by the herte" (III, 1071) and again falls unconscious:

> Therwith the sorwe so his herte shette*   *shut
> That from his eyen fil there nought a tere,
> And every spirit his vigour in knette,*   *contracted its force
> So they astoned* or oppressed were.   *surprised
> The felyng of his sorwe, or of his fere,
> Or of aught elles, fled was out of towne;
> And down he fel al sodeynly a-swowne. (III, 1086–92)

Feeling is acutely embodied and overwhelming, conveyed through the depiction of the closing heart, the withdrawal of spirits astounded by sudden affect, the numbing of the senses, and the resulting swoon.[23] In a characteristically Chaucerian shift in tone, the medical emphasis is comically reiterated when Pandarus and Criseyde chafe Troilus's pulse and palms until breath returns.

The affects of Troilus's love, written on the body in sorrowful sighs, tears and swoons, and in the burning fire of love, are intensified in the later books. On hearing that Criseyde is to be sent to the Greek camp in exchange for the prisoner Antenor, Troilus is possessed by "furie" and "rage" (IV, 253) that express themselves in frenzy or "woodnesse [madness]" (IV, 238). This madness has none of the wilful verbosity of Hamlet's. The affects of the spirits rushing out from Troilus's heart are so extreme that his behaviour resembles that of a wild bull "idarted to the herte" (IV, 240); he rushes round the room, striking his breast, beating his head against the wall and the ground. The violent movement of breath outwards is reflected not only in Troilus's actions but also his roaring out of his complaint. At last the frenzy "that his herte twiste and faste threste" is replaced by grief, his tears accompanied by "[a] thousand sikes, hotter than the gleede [glowing coal]" that release the overheated heart (IV, 254, 337). Eventually, however, this results in overcooling, as too much heat is lost: "so his peynes hym torente [tore him], / And wex so mat [exhausted/dejected], that joie nor penaunce / He feleth non, but lith forth in a traunce" (IV, 341–43). Breath has left his lungs and he becomes inanimate; Pandarus's own heart grows cold in sympathy (IV, 362). The focus on heartsickness and its affects is sustained and enhanced as Troilus waits for Criseyde to return as she has promised: his "maladie" is such that he believes he cannot live (V, 316); he experiences a "tremour ... aboute his herte" (V, 255). As her betrayal becomes apparent, physical affect is so extreme that, like Arcite's, Troilus' appearance is dramatically changed:

> He so defet* was, that no manere man   *enfeebled
> Unneth* hym myghte knowen ther he wente;   *scarcely
> So was he lene, and therto pale and wan,
> And feble, that he walketh by potente.*   *crutch
> (V, 1219–22)

Again, the heart is the focus: "He seyde his harm was al aboute his herte" (V, 1225). Chaucer medicalises and extends Boccaccio's conventional imagery of the troubled heart, depicting withdrawal of the spirits of a kind so extreme that the body is unmade.[24]

The physiological model of the spirits and the movement of breath, then, are critical to Chaucer's depiction of emotional experience as a deeply embodied phenomenon. One effect of this model is to identify the lover as sufferer in two senses—as suffering the pains of love, but also as suffering or acted upon by the passions, and in this sense as *passive*. The passivity of feeling, weeping, sighing, swooning is mitigated by an emphasis on cognition, recognition, knowing and making sense of emotional experience. In Chaucer's male lovers, it is also mitigated by an emphasis on prowess and chivalry: Arcite and Palamon are first encountered on the battlefield, and enact their rivalry through both their battle in the forest and the great tournament that concludes the tale; Troilus rides through the streets of Troy in triumph after battle, his chivalric excellence increases through love, and he is eventually killed on the battlefield. While we only see the Man in Black as suffering lover, he is allusively identified as John of Gaunt; the narrator's mode of address places him as feudal lord, and it is evident from his narrative that he actively fulfils this role. Action of this kind, however, is denied Chaucer's female victims of love, and it is striking that in relation to his depiction of female protagonists, Chaucer is careful to balance his depiction of the body overcome by suffering with an emphasis on agency. Breath and the movement of the spirits play essential roles in demonstrating truly felt emotion and virtue, but they are balanced by the exercise of free will and thought-through choice.

Chaucer's *Man of Law's Tale* exemplifies his treatment of breath in relation to female protagonists. The tale is haunted by the image of Custance's "deedly pale face" (822). Accused of murder and led through the streets, her pallour provides physical evidence of the withdrawal of the vital spirits through fear: "Have ye nat seyn somtyme a pale face ... ?" (645) Her immediate response to the murder of her host's wife is to swoon: "For verray wo hir wit was al aweye" (609). The withdrawal of vital spirits and hence of animal spirits in the brain prevents the working of "wit," the inner senses. Yet Chaucer is also careful to emphasise Custance's agency: the withdrawal of vital spirits—air and blood—is balanced by control when she is publicly accused of murder: "So stant Custance, and looketh hire aboute" (651). Exiled on the sea, she is not portrayed as a swooning victim but from the start "taketh in good entente / The wyl of Crist" (824–25). By contrast, at her reunion with her husband, affect is written on her body in the most extreme terms: "she, for sorwe, as doumb stant as a tree, / So was hir herte shet in hir distresse / Whan she remembred his unkyndenesse. / Twyes she swowned in his owene sighte" (1055–58). As with Chaucer's portrayals of male lovers, the imagery of the heart closing is physiologically acute: Custance swoons repeatedly as the spirits withdraw, her response reflected in her husband's swoons and tears. Now it is as if affect is released by the restoration of natural order and justice. In contrast, Chaucer's contemporary John Gower, who uses some of the same legends in his *Confessio Amantis*, an extended story collection exemplifying the seven deadly sins in relation to love, chooses to emphasise the movement of the spirits more consistently, particularly through the response of swooning. In Gower's extended narrative of Constance, intensely felt affect and the accompanying loss of breath are emphasised in relation to suffering: on discovering the dead Hermengyld, Constance lies "swounende ded for fere … stille as eny Ston."[25] Gower's Constance, cast out in her rudderless ship, evokes pity precisely through the extremes of her physical response: she lies "[s]wounende as ded" (II, 1063). Feeling is physically manifest in the movement of the vital spirits and breath—the swoon and the rush of tears, which are contrasted by her prayer for her child and return to strength. Again in opposition to Chaucer's account, however, at the denouement Gower offers no detail concerning Constance's response: here his interest is in the affects of recognition and reunion experienced by the male lover, whose predicament in some sense chimes with that of his narrator and alter ego, Amans.

Chaucer's *Legend of Good Women* engages most extensively with the experience of tragic female love, though the tone of its series of classical legends, purportedly written to demonstrate female virtue, is notoriously ambiguous. The women of the *Legend* can seem troublingly passive, repeatedly written out in death, yet Chaucer's realisation of the interconnected workings of mind, body and affect also affords its subjects individuality and agency. The physiology of grief provides Chaucer with the means to explore natural feeling and virtue. Thus Thisbe's heart pounds with emotion: "like the wawes quappe gan hire herte" (865); she grows as pale as boxwood. The withdrawal of vital spirits is made visible in her pallour, swoon and tears, so that, like the Man in Black, she becomes a living emblem of grief. Whereas Aeneas's falseness is reflected in the unnatural division between body and mind, so that his countenance belies his intention, Dido manifests intense grief: as the vital spirits are sent back from the arteries into the heart, "[t]wenty tyme yswouned hath she thanne" (1342). Ariadne's heart similarly grows "cold" (2197), while Hypsipyle's grief at Jason's betrayal is the most extreme manifestation of the withdrawal of vital spirits and breath: she "deyede for his love, of sorwes smerte" (1579).

In the *Legend*, embodied emotion is also true, virtuous emotion, contrasting with the feigned emotion of men. Its physiological basis underwrites that truth, taking emotional experience beyond convention. Yet extreme physical affects are also, as in the *Man of Law's Tale*, employed selectively, particularly in relation to suicide, which is repeatedly depicted as a conscious choice. The play of breath at the last is consciously orchestrated. Thus Cleopatra's, Thisbe's, Phyllis' and Dido's deaths are carefully thought-through actions. Cleopatra responds to her "sorweful herte" not by swooning but by fulfilling the covenant she has made to feel the same "wel or wo" as Anthony (681, 689). Thisbe's "drery herte" fuels the act that proves "[a] woman dar and can as wel" as a man: "My woful hand ... / Is strong ynogh" (810, 923, 890–91). Dido's embodiment of grief is replaced by her carefully reasoned suicide, enacted with Aeneas's sword, and allowing time for prayer and lament. Chaucer controls affective extremes to highlight free will and agency, in particular, in relation to the choice of when and how to take the last breath. Whereas Chaucer balances affect with control to suggest agency, Gower's renditions of the same legends emphasise the power of affect over rationality. Thus his Thisbe swoons on finding Piramus's body, a "traunce" (III, 1447) that embodies extreme grief: she regains her breath only to voice her final lament. Death results from the sorrow which "overgoth hire wittes" (III, 1488)—a brief evocation of the withdrawal of the spirits—in contrast to the reasoned suicide of Chaucer's Thisbe. Suicide, for Gower, is the ultimate expression of extreme grief, an act of the body bereft of reason. Though in the *Confessio* Dido's death is recounted only briefly, with the emphasis placed on her complaint, the enduring image is of frenzied grief, that of the swan who drives a feather into her brain for sorrow.

In Chaucer's legend of Lucrece, the movement of the vital spirits and the play of breath fulfil their most critical function, proving Lucrece's innocence in relation to her rape, a subject extensively debated by medieval theologians from Augustine onwards.[26] Fear of the rapist Tarquinius paralyses Lucrece's cognitive processes through withdrawal of vital spirits and hence of animal spirits: "Hire wit is al ago" (1797). Chaucer compares her response to that of animals frozen in terror, as is the lamb in the claws of the wolf. The extreme affects of fear preclude any possibility of collusion by causing the complete withdrawal of the vital spirits into the heart: "what for fer of sclaunder and drede of deth, / She loste bothe at ones wit and breth ... . / She feleth no thyng, neyther foul ne fayr" (1814–18). Critical views placing Lucrece's swoon as symbolic of the failure of agency do not take account of medieval models of the physiology of emotion, the affective movement that leaves the body without "wit and breth." Chaucer's phrasing underlines the swoon's origin in the constraint of vital spirits and accompanying loss of breath.

2 THE PLAY OF BREATH: CHAUCER'S NARRATIVES OF FEELING

Paradoxically, passivity is rooted in the extreme action of the spirits, and proves steadfastness and "trouthe" (1860). Lucrece's swoon contrasts physically with the rushing out of Tarquinius's overheated vital spirits from his fiery heart (1751), which leads him to enact his desire. Lucrece's suicide, by contrast, is a deeply reasoned action, described through strikingly active language: "she rafte hirself hir lyf" (1855). Chaucer's final emphasis is on her conscious steadfastness of mind, manifest in her fixed will: "Ne in hir wille she chaunged for no newe" (1875). The moment that breath is lost in self-inflicted death also proves "the stable herte, sadde and kynde" (1876). Gower adopts the same defence in relating the story of Lucrece. In his narrative, the withdrawal of spirits to the heart is an expression of femininity: she "thurgh tendresce of wommanhiede / Hire vois hath lost for pure drede" (VII, 4975–76). Like Chaucer's Lucrece, she is redeemed from any accusation of guilt: she "swounede" and "lay ded oppressed" (VII, 4986–87); Gower's physiological detail, however, is notably less, and he does not explore the rational, volitional aspects of suicide.

Chaucer's *Legend of Good Women* concludes with legend of Hypermnestra, whose femininity is defined by her inability to take up male weapons and commit murder. Chaucer memorably evokes the withdrawal of vital spirits: "As cold as any frost now waxeth she; / For pite by the herte hire streyneth so" (2683–84); she weeps and shakes, swooning three times. Regaining consciousness, she recognises violence as antithetical to her gender: "I am a mayde, and, as by my nature, / And bi my semblaunt and by my vesture, / Myne handes ben nat shapen for a knyf" (2690–92). The tale is incomplete, breaking off with Hypermnestra's imprisonment, and Chaucer emphasises her vulnerability: "This sely woman is so weik – Allas! / And helples" (2713–14). Yet if she is the archetypal female victim, it is also striking that precisely the extremes of affect reflected in loss of breath and in the swoon bring her to the realisation of her nature and the defence of *trouthe*. In her seeming passivity and refusal to act, Hypermnestra also exercises agency and free will. The movement of breath causing unconsciousness inspires conscious choice and assertion of the will.

Engagement with the play of breath, the precise physiology of the vital spirits that governs the emotions and the power of affect over body and mind, then, allows Chaucer to dramatise the physicality of intense experience and the embodied quality of emotion, to probe the intersections of virtue and feeling, to explore questions of agency and to illuminate the intimate connections between mind, body and affect. Romance structures and their conventions have their own spiritual force: they work to evoke and to animate the textures of human experience, of thinking, feeling and breathing in the world.

Notes

1. James (1912, 36–37).
2. Ibid., 37.
3. This essay draws on research undertaken for the "Life of Breath" (http://www.lifeofbreath.org/) project, generously funded by a Wellcome Trust Senior Investigator Award (WT098455MA). It is also indebted to research undertaken for "Hearing the Voice" (http://hearingthevoice.org/), funded by a Wellcome Trust Strategic Award (WT086049) and Collaborative Award (WT108720). I am very grateful to the Trust for their support of my research and to my colleagues for their insights. See also my essay "Mind, Breath and Voice in Chaucer's Romance Writing", in Hilger, ed. (2017, 119–141). I am grateful to the editor for permission to draw on this material here.
4. On medieval medicine, see further Cameron (1993), Getz (1998), Rawcliffe (1995), Rubin (1974), Siraisi (1990) and Talbot (1967).
5. Porter (1997, 77). For an extensive study of theories of *pneuma* in classical philosophy and medicine, and in early Christian thought, see Verbeke (1945), and further on classical thought, van der Eijk (2005, 119–135).
6. Ibid., 76–77. On medieval theories of the brain, see Harvey (1975) and Avicenna (1968).
7. Isidore of Seville (2006, XI.i.124).
8. Further on Constantine's *Pantegni*, see Burnett and Jacquart, ed. (1994).
9. Bartholomaeus Anglicus, trans. Trevisa (1975, III.15, vol. 1, 104–105); for the Latin, see Bartholomaeus Anglicus (1979, 35–36).
10. Isidore of Seville (2006, XI.1.7).
11. Grudzen (2007, 63–64, 200–201).
12. Richard Rolle (1972, 45); for the original see Rolle (1915, 145).
13. James (1884, 189–190), and see Damasio (2000, 2006). On theories of the emotions in classical and medieval philosophy, see Knuuttila (2004) and Pickavé and Shapiro, ed. (2012).
14. See *Oxford English Dictionary*, sigh, *n.* 1, sigh *v.* 1a., 2a., 3b.; swoon, *n.*, 1a., 1b; swoon *v.*, 1a, 2; *Middle English Dictionary*, swŏugh, *n.*, 1, 2.
15. On the swoon as caused by "strong emotional disturbance" affecting the spirits and by sexual deprivation, see Weiss (2011, 133); on literary swoons see Windeatt (2011).
16. *Parliament of Fowls*, in Chaucer (1987, lines 246–250). All subsequent references to Chaucer's works are to this edition, cited by line number.

17. On medical writings on lovesickness from Constantine's *Viaticum* onwards, see Wack (1990).
18. Chaucer's Prologue to *The Legend of Good Women* refers to his translation of the *Roman de la Rose*. Three fragments of a Middle English *Romaunt of the Rose* survive, attributed to Chaucer in Thynne's sixteenth-century edition; of these only Fragment A (cited here and perhaps written early in his career) is now thought to be Chaucer's, though critical debate continues.
19. On the psychological physiology of the heart and reception of these ideas in England from the twelfth century onwards, see Metlitzki (2005, 64–73).
20. Keats (1970, 539, lines 9–10).
21. See Bartholomaeus Anglicus, trans. Trevisa (1975, VII.6, vol. 1, 350): the passage instances "grete þou3tes of sorwe, and of to greet studie, and of drede," but not love; for the Latin see Bartholomaeus Anglicus (1964, VII.6).
22. See Bartholomaeus Anglicus, trans. Trevisa (1975, III.8, III.12, vol. 1, 97, 99); for the Latin see Bartholomaeus Anglicus (1979, 28, 30). On this passage, see Chaucer (1987, *Knight's Tale* 2749), explanatory note; and further Aiken (1936) and Curry (1960, 139–145).
23. On Troilus as swooning "in part because of an as-yet unfulfilled sexual life," rather than simply through heightened emotional sensitivity, see Weiss (2011, 133).
24. For a parallel text presenting Boccaccio's *Il Filostrato* alongside Chaucer's *Troilus and Criseyde*, see Chaucer (1984).
25. Gower (1990, 1991, II, 846–847). All subsequent references to the *Confessio Amantis* will be to this edition, cited by book and line number.
26. See further Saunders (2001, 152–177, 267–273).

References

Aiken, Pauline. 1936. Arcite's Illness and Vincent of Beauvais. *PMLA* 51: 361–369.

Avicenna. 1968. *Liber de anima seu Sextus de naturalibus*, ed. Simone van Riet. Leiden: Brill.

Bartholomaeus Anglicus. 1964 [1601]. *De rerum proprietatibus*. Frankfurt: Minerva.

Bartholomaeus Anglicus. 1975. *On the Properties of Things: John of Trevisa's Translation of Bartholomaeus Anglicus De Proprietatibus Rerum*, vol. 3, ed. M.C. Seymour. Oxford: Oxford University Press.

Bartholomaeus Anglicus. 1979. *On the Properties of Soul and Body. De Proprietatibus Rerum Libri III et IV*, ed. R. James Long. Toronto Medieval Latin Texts. Toronto: Centre for Medieval Studies and Pontifical Institute of Mediaeval Studies.

Burnett, Charles, and Danielle Jacquart (eds.). 1994. *Constantine the African and ʿAlī Ibn Al-ʿAbbās Al-Maǧūsī: The "Pantegni" and Related Texts*. Studies in Ancient Medicine 10. Leiden: Brill.

Cameron, M.L. 1993. *Anglo-Saxon Medicine*. Cambridge: Cambridge University Press.

Chaucer, Geoffrey. 1984. *Troilus and Criseyde: A New Edition of "The Book of Troilus"*, ed. B.A. Windeatt. London: Longman.

Chaucer, Geoffrey. 1987. *The Riverside Chaucer*, ed. Larry D. Benson. Oxford: Oxford University Press.

Curry, Walter Clyde. 1960. *Chaucer and the Mediaeval Sciences*. New York: Barnes and Noble.

Damasio, Antonio. 2000. *The Feeling of What Happens: Body, Emotion and the Making of Consciousness*. London: Vintage.

Damasio, Antonio. 2006 [1994]. *Descartes' Error: Emotion, Reason and the Human Brain*. London: Vintage.

Getz, Faye. 1998. *Medicine in the English Middle Ages*. Princeton: Princeton University Press.

Gower, John. 1900, 1901. *Confessio Amantis: The English Works of John Gower*, vol. 2, ed. G.C. Macaulay. Early English Text Society, ES 81 and 82. London: Oxford University Press.

Grudzen, Gerald J. 2007. *Medical Theory About the Body and the Soul in the Middle Ages: The First Western Medical Curriculum at Monte Cassino*. Lewiston: Edwin Mellen Press.

Harvey, Ruth. 1975. *The Inward Wits: Psychological Theory in the Middle Ages and the Renaissance*. London: Warburg Institute, University of London.

Hilger, Stephanie M. (ed.). 2017. *New Directions in Literature and Medicine Studies*. London: Palgrave Macmillan.

Isidore of Seville. 2006. *The Etymologies of Isidore of Seville*, trans. Stephen A. Barney, W.J. Lewis, J.A. Beach, Oliver Berghof, with Muriel Hall. Cambridge: Cambridge University Press.

James, William. 1884. What Is an Emotion? *Mind* 9: 188–205.

James, William. 1912. What Is Consciousness? In *Essays in Radical Empiricism*, ed. Ralph Barton Perry, 1–38. New York: Longmans, Green.

Keats, John. 1970. *The Poems of John Keats*, ed. Miriam Allott. Longman Annotated English Poets. London: Longman.

Knuuttila, Simo. 2004. *Emotions in Ancient and Medieval Philosophy*. Oxford: Oxford University Press.

Metlitzki, Dorothee. 2005. *The Matter of Araby in Medieval England*. New Haven: Yale University Press.

Pickavé, Martin, and Lisa Shapiro (eds.). 2012. *Emotion and Cognitive Life in Medieval and Early Modern Philosophy*. Oxford: Oxford University Press.

Porter, Roy. 1997. *The Greatest Benefit to Mankind: A Medical History of Humanity from Antiquity to the Present*. London: HarperCollins.
Rawcliffe, Carole. 1995. *Medicine and Society in Later Medieval England*. Stroud: Sutton.
Rolle, Richard. 1915. *The "Incendium Amoris" of Richard Rolle of Hampole*, ed. Margaret Deanesley. Manchester: Manchester University Press.
Rolle, Richard. 1972. *The Fire of Love*, trans. Clifton Wolters. Harmondsworth: Penguin.
Rubin, Stanley. 1974. *Medieval English Medicine*. New York: Barnes and Noble.
Saunders, Corinne. 2001. *Rape and Ravishment in the Literature of Medieval England*. Cambridge: D.S. Brewer.
Siraisi, Nancy G. 1990. *Medieval and Early Renaissance Medicine: An Introduction to Knowledge and Practice*. Chicago: University of Chicago Press.
Talbot, C.H. 1967. *Medicine in Medieval England*. London: Oldbourne.
van der Eijk, Philip J. 2005. *Medicine and Philosophy in Classical Antiquity: Doctors and Philosophers on Nature, Soul, Health and Disease*. Cambridge: Cambridge University Press.
Verbeke, G. 1945. *L'Évolution de la doctrine du pneuma du stoïcisme à S. Augustin, étude philosophique*. Bibliothèque de l'Institut Supérieur de Philosophie, Université de Louvain. Paris: Desclée de Brouwer.
Wack, Mary. 1990. *Lovesickness in the Middle Ages: The Viaticum and Its Commentaries*. Philadelphia: University of Pennsylvania Press.
Weiss, Judith. 2011. Modern and Medieval Views on Swooning: The Literary and Medical Contexts of Fainting in Romance. In *Medieval Romance, Medieval Contexts*, ed. Rhiannon Purdie and Michael Cichon, 121–134. Studies in Medieval Romance. Cambridge: D.S. Brewer.
Windeatt, Barry. 2011. The Art of Swooning in Middle English. In *Medieval Latin and Middle English Literature: Essays in Honour of Jill Mann*, ed. Christopher Cannon and Maura Nolan, 211–230. Cambridge: D.S. Brewer.

Open Access This chapter is licensed under the terms of the Creative Commons Attribution 4.0 International License (http://creativecommons.org/licenses/by/4.0/), which permits use, sharing, adaptation, distribution and reproduction in any medium or format, as long as you give appropriate credit to the original author(s) and the source, provide a link to the Creative Commons license and indicate if changes were made.

The images or other third party material in this chapter are included in the chapter's Creative Commons license, unless indicated otherwise in a credit line to the material. If material is not included in the chapter's Creative Commons license and your intended use is not permitted by statutory regulation or exceeds the permitted use, you will need to obtain permission directly from the copyright holder.

CHAPTER 3

Wasting Breath in *Hamlet*

Naya Tsentourou

Abstract This chapter draws on instances of disordered breathing in *Hamlet* in order to examine the cultural significance of sighs in the early modern period, as well as in the context of current work in the field of medical humanities. Tracing the medical history of sighing in ancient and early modern treatises of the passions, the chapter argues that sighs, in the text and the performance of the tragedy, exceed their conventional interpretation as symptoms of pain and disrupt meaning on the page and on stage. In the light of New Materialist theory, the air circulating in *Hamlet* is shown to dismantle narratives of representation, posing new questions for the future of medical humanities.

Keywords *Hamlet* · Sighs · Breath · Air · Emotions · Medical humanities

> CLAUDIUS: There lives within the very flame of love
> A kind of wick or snuff that will abate it;
> And nothing is at a like goodness still;
> For goodness, growing to a pleurisy,
> Dies in his own too-much. That we would do,
> We should do when we would; for this 'would' changes,
> And hath abatements and delays as many
> As there are tongues, are hands, are accidents,
> And then this 'should' is like a spendthrift's sigh
> That hurts by easing. But to the quick of th'ulcer.
> (4.7.112–21, Appendix A in the Oxford edition)

Delivered in conspiratorial confidence by Claudius to Laertes, urging him to avenge the death of Polonius by murdering Hamlet in a fatal duel, these lines appear in the second quarto of *Hamlet* (1604) but are removed from the First Folio edition (1623) of the play. According to the Oxford editor, G.R. Hibbard, "the excision of these lines from F is a gain" as they unnecessarily prolong Claudius's interrogation of Laertes's intentions and his insistence on ensuring the wronged son's commitment to revenge. While the extract might be superfluous to the progress of the play's performance, the lines remain faithful to the tragedy's preoccupation with excess of passion, and its potential to consume the individual incapable of moderation.[1] The moral imperative to revenge is communicated via means of popular knowledge: editors are quick to acknowledge that the phrase "like a spendthrift's sigh / that hurts by easing" refers to the idea "that every sigh a man breathes costs him a drop of blood and thus wastes part of his life."[2] The folkloric origins of the concept are generally adopted by editions of the play as early as the eighteenth century, with Samuel Johnson glossing the line as "a *sigh* that makes an unnecessary waste of the vital flame. It is a notion very prevalent, that *sighs* ... wear out the animal powers."[3] Moreover, editors are often prone to draw on other examples from the Shakespearean canon where sighing is perceived as consuming blood: we find cross-references to *2 Henry 6* with sighs described as "blood-consuming" and "blood-drinking" (3.2. 60–4), to *3 Henry 6*, where sighs are called "blood-sucking" (4.5. 21–4), and to *A Midsummer Night's Dream* where "sighs of love cost the fresh blood dear" (3.2. 97).[4] While they agree on the cultural capital of the phrase, editors disagree on whether the line in *Hamlet* should read a "spendthrift's sigh" or "a spendthrift sigh." In the first case, advocated by the Arden editors and found in the original quarto, the sigh refers to the prodigal man's regret of having spent his money. In the second case, adopted by Hibbard, the sigh itself is the spendthrift, problematising a figurative reading and raising questions about bodies and their potential to self-destruct.[5]

Even as Claudius projects a distant and undefinable future where Laertes's sigh becomes a synonym of regret, physiological sighs are absent from the stage. The king digresses, wasting breath and words, having to recollect himself and resume focus "to the quick of th'ulcer." The textual reference to sighing does not record a symptom or incite a stage direction, as is often the case in the play; the sigh here is positioned between the physiological and the emotional, yet escapes both by being proverbial. It has been rendered axiomatic, validated by observations of both the expelled air and its wasteful effect on the suffering individual. At the same time, it has transformed into shared medical knowledge derived culturally and transmitted on and off stage via Shakespeare, his characters and his editors. Its encyclopaedic aura is of the empirical style found in a treatise like Francis Bacon's *Sylva Sylvarum* (1627), where sighing is defined as "caused by the drawing in of a greater quantity of breath to refresh the heart that laboureth: like a great draught when one is thirsty."[6] Claudius, like another natural philosopher or physician, has assigned meaning to his observations which he has fixed with a simile allowing no deviation between points A and B of the comparison, and is reiterating common knowledge on disrupted patterns of breathing. Shakespeare's editors, comparing the lines to other instances of wasteful sighs in Shakespeare, follow suit.

The proverbial waste of the body is one of the narrative ways in which the play figures and reconfigures disrupted breathing. In other instances, sighs communicate emotional states such as grief and pain, the exaggerated rhetoric and theatricality of a lover, and, ultimately, the final moments of one's life. In the second part of the chapter, I show how the deeply inhaled and exhaled air, which, according to Claudius, "hurts by easing," blurring pain with relief and cause with remedy, destabilises in the process the very narratives it seeks to validate. In examining how disrupted breath dismantles representation, my underlying question, arising in the context of this volume and in its engagement with medical humanities, shifts from "*what* can sighing mean?" to "*how* does sighing mean?" on stage and in early modern scientific circles.

My analysis of sighing in *Hamlet* is informed by the revisionist agenda of New Materialism and the model of entanglement that accompanies its recent adoption by scholars of the history of emotions and the Critical Medical Humanities alike. In the last two decades, New Materialism has begun to (re)adjust humanist and social constructivist theories and practices that have emphasised human agency, or the lack thereof, and have reproduced rigid boundaries between nature and culture, and between human and non-human matter.[7] Influential voices, such as Karen Barad, object to materialist discourse (including Foucault's and Butler's) which delineates matter to a definitive and measurable existence or apparatus, carefully separated from and existing outside the realm of human activity, language and behaviour. For Barad, "matter is neither fixed and given nor the mere end result of different processes. Matter is produced and productive, generated and generative. Matter is agentive, not a fixed essence or property of things."[8] When Gertrude sighs at the beginning of Act 4 in *Hamlet*, Claudius's adoption of an external observation point to evaluate the "matter" of her breathing ("There's matter in these sighs, these profound heaves; / You must translate. 'Tis fit we understand them" [4.1. 1–2]) proves inadequate. The king seeks to immediately place Gertrude's audibly and visually distressed body within an epistemological framework that will explain her sighs and what they represent. His project is one of urgent translation: of transporting the sighs from the world of things to the world of words, despite Gertrude's insistence in the scene directly preceding Claudius' entry that "if words be made of breath / And breath of life, I have no life to breathe / What thou hast said to me" (3.4. 195–7).[9] For the New Materialist Barad, the representationalism Claudius perpetuates is characteristic of Newtonian metaphysical individualism and humanism and "never seems to get any closer to solving the problem it poses because it is caught in the impossibility of stepping outward from its metaphysical starting place."[10] Likewise, Gertrude's embodiment of frantic breathing on stage cannot be observed from a privileged exterior position; her sighs are neither only words nor only things: "things don't pre-exist ... outside of particular agential intra-actions, 'words' and 'things' are indeterminate. Matter is therefore not to be understood as a property of things but, like discursive practices, must be understood in more dynamic and productive terms – in terms of intra-activity."[11] How we might resist the humanist temptation to quantify and account for sighs in strictly representational terms, and how, on the other hand, we might *feel* them as phenomena that performatively iterate their materiality are the driving concerns of this chapter.[12]

Intra-activity in *Hamlet* complicates and implicates the material existence of audience and actors, of observers and performers, of the theatre and the world. Emotional breathing escapes the confines of the dramatic text and flows between page, stage and audience in unpredictable, yet inclusive, circles. Breath belongs to, and is determined by, the affective fabric of the original playtext as much as it is by the actor's present and living body, while the recycling process of inhaling and exhaling reaches out to implicate the spectators, whom, according to Carolyn Sale, breath animates: "what they receive renders them active, or rather creates in them the capacity or the potential to become that which they observe: the breath makes them 'capable' by turning them all into potential actors."[13] Carolyn Sale and Carla Mazzio both draw on the materiality of air and breath in their analyses of *Hamlet*. Mazzio argues that the word "matter" in Claudius's command maintains its definition as substance, and specifically, "air": "an element packed with atoms … a medium through which other elements … could move or be moved … a central medium of intellection and communication."[14] In a tour-de-force analysis of the history of air in and through *Hamlet*, Mazzio examines how Renaissance artists, including Shakespeare, Dürer and Donne, negotiated their physical existence and their art in a world whose air was as inspiring as it was vertiginous in a period that prefigured the Enlightenment's quest for conquering air via an array of scientific instruments. The technologies that sought to master air are for Mazzio kin to "an aesthetics of affect [that] emerged out of, and often managed to displace concerns about, the otherwise threatening power of an element that could not be directly seen, understood, controlled, or subjected to 'capture.'"[15] Sale transfers the discussion of the physics and metaphysics of air back to the materiality of the Renaissance stage, outlining a theory of performance that rests on the transmission of breath between actors and audiences "in a play so insistently about the material."[16] Mazzio's and Sale's studies, however, tend to re-inscribe the boundaries they aim to interrogate, treating the matter of air as a separate, albeit circulating, substance, impacting on the cultural parameters of the age and the stage. In what follows, I will reformulate their historical materialism with the aim to articulate "active process[es] of materialization of which embodied humans are an integral part, rather than the monotonous repetitions of dead matter from which human subjects are apart."[17]

Reading breath in *Hamlet*, and sighing in particular, as "dead matter" which the human participants of a performance re-enact and put to use reduces it to an instrumental role that obscures its "vitality," "preventing us from detecting (seeing, hearing, smelling, tasting, feeling) a fuller range of the nonhuman powers circulating around and within human bodies."[18] The character of Hamlet, aware of the potential of his own body to be used as a vessel for one's breath and to serve the purposes of others, refutes the instrumentalisation of air matter.

> HAMLET: It is as easy as lying. Govern these ventages with your fingers and thumb, give it breath with your mouth, and it will discourse most eloquent music. Look you, these are the stops.
> ...
> You would play upon me! You would seem to know my stops, you would pluck out the heart of my mystery, you would sound me from my lowest note to my compass. And there is much music, excellent voice, in this little organ. Yet cannot you make it speak. 'Sblood! Do you think I am easier to be played on than a pipe? Call me what instrument you will, though you fret me you cannot play upon me. (3.2. 349–63)

In exposing the scheming intentions of his childhood friends, Rosencrantz and Guildenstern, and refusing to act as the pipe into which air will be passively channelled and invested with external meaning, Hamlet resists the assumption that breath is the mere manipulation of air. One of the first things we learn about Hamlet is that he does not waste sighs in vain, and is indeed wary of those who use their breath in instructed and artificial ways. He states so in his first appearance, where he enlists breathlessness as an actor's tool.

> HAMLET: Seems, madam – nay, it is, I know not 'seems'.
> 'Tis not alone my inky cloak, cold mother,
> Nor customary suits of solemn black,
> Nor windy suspiration of forced breath,
> No, nor the fruitful river in the eye,
> Nor the dejected haviour of the visage,
> Together with all forms, moods, shapes of grief
> That can denote me truly. These indeed 'seem',
> For they are actions that a man might play,
> But I have that within which passes show,
> These but the trappings and the suits of woe. (1.2. 76–86)

Listing what "seems" against "that within which passes show" Hamlet condemns the validity of the performative elements of grief, from funereal garments and material accessories to mournful physical expressions, including the "windy suspiration of forced breath." The *Oxford English Dictionary* marks Hamlet's comment here as the first example where the term "suspiration" refers to "(deep) breathing."[19] In his sarcastic rejection of what he perceives to be Gertrude and Claudius's feigned sorrow, Hamlet chooses to emphasise grief's manifestation through corporal air, resulting in and from sighs, by drawing attention to its evaporating and insubstantial nature. The compressed circulation and expulsion of air from the body is identified as a universal symptom of grief, but the double meanings in "windy" (relating to the wind and frivolous, bombastic and unsubstantial) and in "forced" (violently expelled and feigned), as well as the context of Hamlet's speech, render breathlessness insincere. Hamlet's response undermines the validity of forced breath as a symptom, as a sign on which we can fix meaning and put order to an experience, try to understand it, reset and refresh it.

Hamlet's rejection of the distancing effect of this kind of representation contrasts with one of the most affective moments in the tragedy, where the wasteful energy of suspiration is securely (though falsely) embraced in Ophelia's account of Hamlet's appearance in her closet, reported to Polonius in Act 2, Scene 1:

> OPHELIA: ...
> At last, a little shaking of mine arm
> And thrice his head thus waving up and down,
> He raised a sigh so piteous and profound
> As it did seem to shatter all his bulk
> And end his being. (2.1. 89–93)

Ophelia's lines are delivered in a state of shock and apparent distress after her meeting with Hamlet: she enters the scene "affrighted" (2.1. 72) and "fear[s]" (2.1. 82) Hamlet has gone mad. Whether the part is performed in a frantic or stunned manner, her report carries an emotional intensity that in most productions is interpolated with her disrupted breaths (due to haste of delivery and/or edginess), and makes the encounter vivid in the audience's mind. Although we can only imagine Hamlet's sigh, directors might opt for Ophelia to embody in her gestures the sigh that shutters Hamlet. Both Katie West, in Sarah Frankcom's *Hamlet* (Royal Exchange, Manchester, 2014), and Natalie Simpson, in Simon Godwin's production (RSC, Stratford-Upon-Avon, 2016), for instance, pointed to their stomach with tense hand gestures as they brought that sigh to life, a nod perhaps to the notion prevalent in the period that bowels are "the seat of the tender and sympathetic emotions."[20] The wasting of blood Claudius mentions to Laertes is here reinvented as the emptying and annihilation of the body, an inevitable effect of turbulent sighing, leading Polonius to declare his verdict:

> POLONIUS: ...
> This is the very ecstasy of love,
> Whose violent property fordoes itself
> And leads the will to desperate undertakings
> As oft as any passions under heaven
> That does afflict our natures. (2.1. 99–103)

That the body appears to be wasting itself in sighing allows Polonius to offer a satisfactory, for his purposes, explanation and to categorise Hamlet's breath under passionate, and thus violent, love melancholy. Hamlet's, and Ophelia's for that matter, disordered state is neatly regulated by her father, who seeks to make known what he perceives is hidden in Hamlet's interior: "This must be known which, being kept close, might move / More grief to hide than hate to utter love" (2.1. 115–16). Polonius has created a narrative out of the loss of air that Hamlet purportedly performs via Ophelia's body and account.

Constructing narratives of sighing as wasteful yet restorative has been a traditional practice of the health sciences from antiquity to the twenty-first century. In early medical theory, sighing is benign rather than threatening, its main purpose being to cool and refresh the labouring heart and to revive the vital spirits, becoming a close synonym to respiration in general. Discussions of respiration before the experiments of Boyle and Hooke in the second half of the seventeenth century relied predominantly on Aristotelian and Galenic models of physiology, both classical paradigms that took breathing as a cooling agent for the body's innate heat.[21] In *Timaeus*, one of the earliest Western accounts of the mechanism of respiration, Plato, expanding on Empedocles before him, argued that

> as the heart might be easily raised to too high a temperature by hurtful irritation, the genii placed the lungs in its neighbourhood, which adhere to it and fill the cavity of the thorax, in order that the air vessels might moderate the great heat of that organ, and reduce the vessels to an exact obedience.[22]

Following his example, Aristotle wrote in *On Respiration* that "as the chest rises, the air from outside must flow in, as it does into the bellows, and being cold and refrigerative quench the excess of fire. ... it enters in cold and passes out hot, because of its contact with the heat."[23] For Galen, too, the body's heat can only be "sustained by way of the 'ventilation' of the body due to the influx of the external air's refreshing quality throughout the body."[24] As far as the beginnings of Western physiology are concerned, there seems to be little scientific interest in sighs in particular, but it does appear in discussions of emotions which cause turbulent respiration. As early as the third century BC Alexander of Aphrodisias, a leading Peripatic philosopher and commentator of Aristotle, answering "why doe such as are in griefe, and in love, and in anger, sigh very oft?", argues that a sigh is actually produced when the body, due to excessive passion, forgets to act according to its regular routine:

> Because that the soule and minde of such as are grieved, is turned into the cause of griefe and sorrowe ... the soule then being intentive upon that whither she moveth, doth after a sort neglect & forget to give motive vertue and power unto the muscles of the breast. Therefore the heart not receiving aire by opening of the breast, & by a consequence neither blowing not cooling, ... the heart, I say, doth force the minde and give her warning, that she would give more motion unto the muscles, and cause greater breathing in and out, and that she would take more store of colde ayre, and thrust out more excrements, and that often small breathings would performe that that one great one may effect. And therefore men of oldtime; called the word suspirio sighing, of the straitnes of the breast.[25]

When confronted with and immersed in excessive sorrow or love, sighing is the heart's solution to the negligence and numbness of the mind, seeking to restore the balance that has been disrupted by the stillness of the chest. The body appears to lose its cognitive abilities and to sleep, forgetting itself, until the suffocating heart moves to a sudden motion. The notion that sighing is an impulsive and abrupt movement of the emotionally overwhelmed heart trickles down to the Renaissance and our familiar treatises of passions. These customarily list sighing as a symptom of melancholy, whether in the form of green-sickness or intellectual and religious melancholy. Thomas Wright, for instance, in *The Passions of the Mind* (1604) describes the effects of sadness on the body by suggesting that it floods the heart with melancholy blood and in doing so threatens to dry it: "The cause why sadnesse doth so moove the forces of the body,

I take to be, the gathering together of much melancholy blood about the heart, which collection extinguisheth the good spirits, or at least dulleth them."[26] The dried, dull, contracted heart, lacking moisture, has to sigh, as Timothy Bright's *Treatise of Melancholie* (1586) affirms: "sighing hath no other cause of moving than to coole and refreshe the hearte, with fresh breath, and pure aire, which is the nourishment and foode of the vital spirites, besides the cooling which the heart it selfe receiveth thereby."[27] Sighs attributed to love melancholy work in similar ways as Nicholas Coeffeteau writes in his *Table of Humane Passions* (1621), reminding us of the self-forgetfulness that Alexander of Aphrodisias talks about:

> His soule that loves intirely, is perpetually imployed in the contemplation of the party beloved, and hath no other thoughts but of his merit, the heate abandoning the parts, and retiring into the braine, leaves the whole body in great distemperature, which corrupting and consuming the whole bloud, makes the face grow pale and wane, causeth the trembling of the heart, breds strange convulsions and retires the spirits … followed with passionate and heart-breaking sighes.[28]

For Jacques Ferrand's *Erotomania* (1640), sighs are symptoms of green-sickness but they also gesture towards a process of recollection, being initiated by "Nature" to rectify the absent-mindedness of "strong Imaginations":

> Sighing is caused in Melancholy Lovers, by reason that they many times forget to draw their breath, being wholy taken up with the strong Imaginations that they have, either in beholding the beauty of their Loves, or else, in their Absence, contemplating on their rare perfections, and contriving the meanes how to compass their Desires. So that at length recollecting themselves, Nature is constrained to draw as much Aire at once, as before it should have done at two or three times. And such a Respiration is called, a Sigh; which is indeed nothing else, but, a doubled Respiration.[29]

In premodern accounts of emotions, sighs are interpreted the moment they are exhaled as solid evidence of a complex and rather violent procedure the body has to undergo to tackle its own dis-ease. Sighing emerges as be the body's natural and instinctive cure, offering relief, comfort ("it may seeme probable that the sobbing and sighing … if they be not vehement and long … drawing in of fresh aire, geue also some comfort") and even pleasure that approximates self-indulgence ("it is certaine, that even in cares and vexation, there is also a content in the teares and sighes wee powre forth for the absence of that wee loue").³⁰

The air that is deeply inhaled and exhaled affords the opportunity to read but also to generate meanings, a performative quality that undercuts the expression of love Polonius matches with sighing. Welcoming Rosencrantz's invitation to the players, Hamlet proclaims that the actor playing "the Lover shall not sigh gratis" (2.2. 319), attesting to voluntary sighing as a rhetorical trope for courtship. In fact, Polonius himself might have this tradition of inauthentic sighing in lovesickness in mind, when, in Act 1, warning Ophelia against accepting Hamlet's promise of love, he instructs her:

> POLONIUS: In few, Ophelia,
> Do not believe his vows, for they are brokers
> Not of that dye which their investments show,
> But mere implorators of unholy suits
> Breathing like sanctified and pious bonds
> The better to beguile. (1.3. 125–30)

Hamlet's personified vows are perceived as assuming a devout and spiritual exterior that is facilitated and communicated to Ophelia via his breath. The textual instability here in "bonds," where the Arden editors read it as "bonds" (i.e. written or verbal promises), but Oxford editors following Theobald who amended it to "bawds" in his 1726 edition, alerts us to breathe as hypocritical both in a religious and in a secular context. On a side note, if we accept the word to be "bawds," the lines open up interesting questions about prostitution and the corruption of air, another central preoccupation of the play that dramatises the "foul and pestilent congregation of vapours" (2.2. 268–9). Moreover, advising Raynold how to engage in espionage of his son, Laertes, Polonius again uses "breath" to refer to hypocritical words and to the spread of unsubstantiated rumours. *Hamlet* the play and Hamlet the protagonist are intrigued by the elusive nature of sighing and suspend uncomplicated readings of the air communicated between bodies. In this respect, the play participates in the construction and production of knowledge of respiration rather than transmit it only. Sighs can be instrumental, hypocritical, self-shattering, emotional, escaping definitions that early modern medical discourses seek to fix by closing the gap between the air that escapes the human body and the inner cause or effect of it.

Current medical research on sighs affirms their dominant function as survival mechanisms that control and regulate the disordered body, and acknowledges their significance as critical for life: "the sigh plays a role in monitoring brain state changes, controlling arousal, and homeostatically regulating breathing variability."[31] In February 2016, biochemists succeeded in isolating the exact part of the brain area controlling the respiratory system that is in charge of sighing, revealing that these "two tiny clusters of nerve cells in the brain's stem … act in response to an unconscious command to reinflate as necessary the myriad tiny sacs in the lungs called alveoli, which control the body's traffic in oxygen and carbon dioxide, and which sometimes collapse."[32] Recently, biologists have been "able to completely eliminate sighing from normal breathing in rodents by ablating the central sigh control circuit: several days after removing sighs, their breathing became irregular, confirming a true necessity of sighing."[33] While the physiological attributes of sighing have been confirmed to the degree that we know we could not survive if we did not sigh at least every five minutes, sighing's relationship to our emotional health is not as straightforward. According to research by a group of psychologists in the last decade, "respiratory variability and psychological states are closely related, supporting the hypothesis that sighing may play an important role as resetter of both."[34] Scientists have examined how "expanding the lungs by sighing causes relief of dyspnea and associated chest tightness and restlessness,"[35] demonstrating that sighing "causes release of physiological and/or psychological tension" and that it helps the body recover from mental stress.[36] They have even observed similarities and differences between spontaneous and instructed sighs in order to test to what extent instructed sighs can be used to replicate the positive effects of relief associated with spontaneous sighing. At the same time, "instructed sighing is generated behaviourally instead of chemically, possibly leading to dysregulation instead of regulation" and proving potentially "maladaptive" while not resulting in release of muscle tension characteristic of spontaneous sighing.[37] Like Bright, who warns against vehement sighs in the Renaissance, writing that, "if they be vehement, then shake they the hart and midriffe too much, and cause a sorenesse about those partes,"[38] these studies find that "although the respiratory system may benefit from sighing, when randomness becomes too high, excessive sighing may disregulate the system."[39]

In their introduction to *The Edinburgh Companion to the Critical Medical Humanities*, Anne Whitehead and Angela Woods assert the importance of bringing the past to bear upon current debates in the health sciences. According to the authors, historical perspectives "offer alternative vantage points from which to view, reflect on and critique the biomedical," "enable us to attend to different forms of qualitative critical thinking – and different ways to sensing our world – that were important in the past and that may remain with us today" and "help us to understand the extended, continual and shifting process of negotiation through which certain objects and practices come to our attention and others fade from view."[40] When premodern theories are placed next to modern scientific investigations of sighs, the separation between "words" and "things," or between human activity and matter, is shown to have persisted. The narrativising of sighs and the pathologising of the body in early modern and modern accounts rely on the observers standing outside suspiration, observing it, measuring it by its effects and experimenting with it. The continuity of interpreting sighs as an activity, a "thing" for which science will supply the words, attests to a reading of the body and its air as objects, not as phenomena.[41] This is disturbingly evident, for example, in research conducted on non-human mammals for the purposes of understanding human emotionality. In their attempt to track sighing's relation to emotion, Li and Yackle include the following case: "when rodents are trained to associate auditory tone with an electric tail shock and a light with the omission of the shock, they sigh more when the omission signal is played during the shock signal, which is interpreted as a sigh of relief."[42] Rodents, sound, light and electric shocks constitute an apparatus that for the scientists "provides an important gateway into understanding how emotional sighs, and therefore emotions, are generated."[43] The human factor in this experiment, while the main target of the research, is reduced to its technological instruments as if absent from the stimuli and conditions the rodents find themselves in. Human emotion is investigated as distinct—mirrored in the emotion of other mammals but not associated with its production.

In the search of scientific evidence for the interaction (as opposed to New Materialism's model of intra-action) between sighs and emotions, boundary-making spreads from the human/animal division to discipline demarcations. One study takes as its starting point the fact that "sighs have inspired philosophers, musicians, and poets for several centuries," listing Shakespeare and Bach as examples of "the artists' early understanding of the deeper nature of the sigh."[44] The article concludes that "one day we as scientists will be able to catch up with the great artists who have long appreciated the important role of the sigh in regulating our emotions."[45] The hailing of the arts as instinctively attuned to the behavioural role of sighs presupposes (a) that the arts allow access to a different type of knowledge than the sciences, and (b) that this knowledge is somewhat covert and ineligible until the sciences "catch up" with measuring it and making it available.[46] "We can trust that Shakespeare already knew that sighs are not just augmented breaths" implies that the playwright knew sighs were more than that, but what "that" might be remains hidden.[47] But what if the question of who (person or discipline) knows what about sighing is irrelevant? Adopting entanglement rather than division as a research model disturbs the dynamic between sighs and emotions, confusing the representational readings of sighing offered by Claudius and Polonius and sought after by sciences. As explored earlier in this chapter, *Hamlet* foregrounds the instability and artificiality of ascribing meaning to the air that escapes the human body. As a result, the "corporeality of emotion," its physiological embodiment by individuals and the language used to express this, loses its privileged position in debates of materiality.[48] What we are left with, instead, is sighing as a phenomenon that enacts the boundaries it is said to signify. It does not tell the story of pain or love or sorrow, it does not reorder and reset a body out of tune, but exceeds these perceived functionalities, intra-acting within bodies, air, stage structures.

Refusing instrumentalisation, breath in theatre enables alternative configurations. On stage, sighing is fake and real at the same time; the air is enacted but it is also organic, produced and productive. Its exploration requires an interdisciplinary and entangled approach, relating to and exceeding the history of emotions, the history of medicine, current biological and psychological insights, as well as the affective technologies Steven Mullaney has used to refer to the stage, thinking of theatre in other words as a key mechanism in generating and transmitting collective emotions, in which we are part of the (theatrical) apparatus, not standing on the edges of it.[49] *Hamlet* does not rest at a definition of sighing as a symptom that accompanies emotional or physical suffering, but offers us an example of sighing as "emotional practice." Anthropologist Monique Scheer, building on the work of William Reddy and Barbara Rosenwein, has historicised emotions by applying Pierre Bourdieu's concept of *habitus*, a "system of cognitive and motivating structures"[50] on which she expands as follows: "people move about in their social environments … in most cases supremely practiced at the subtleties of movement, posture, gesture, and expression that connect them with others as well as communicate to themselves who they are."[51] Sighs, in this respect, which in affect theory would traditionally be classified as "automatic behaviours, reflexes, spontaneous responses," can be "more fruitfully thought of as habits emerging where bodily capacities and cultural requirements meet."[52] What makes "emotional practice" a pertinent designation for sighing is the underlining principle that "the physiological contains both the organic and the social, which cooperate in the production of emotion,"[53] undermining purist attachment to the body as well as social determinism. Entangled materiality in *Hamlet* affirms (while contradicting) Scheer's point that "emotions cannot be conjured out of thin air"[54]; in *Hamlet* they *are* air.

Reformulating the interactive relationship between sighs *and* emotions as the intra-active reality of sighs *entangled with* emotions disrupts the narrative of sighing in the play as restoring meaning or reordering an experience.[55] As we have seen, modern terminology of resetting and reinflating seems to share with Renaissance medical discourse a focus on the reorganisation of the body; a reordering of what has been in disorder that in the process can be either life-threatening or life-affirming. Medical writings on sighing try to reset, regulate, refresh, recover, reinflate and reorganise the emotionally and mentally distressed body. In doing so, scientific discussions of distorted breathing can be thought of as producing a narrative of knowledge that relies on air, or else, on what comes in and out of the body, but does not remain. The symptom, sighing, is revealed to be not only elusive and unfixed (its instability most pronounced in the fact that it is also a cure), but it escapes location in a specific part of the body; it is instead found in the body's waste, in what the body expels and rejects, in what is figured as the outside rather than the inside. The "spendthrift sigh" and Claudius's reference to it in the context of delayed and unsatisfactory action allude to what is no longer there, a "should" that has been supplanted by a "would," an ethical commitment to revenge that has been indefinitely postponed, a sigh that has already been wasted. The breath that regulates simultaneously wastes the human body as Shakespeare's *Richard II* reminds us listing sighs as an abject substance; alongside his tears and groans, sighs control the rhythmic functions of the cyborg human clock into which Richard has transformed:

> RICHARD: I wasted time, and now doth Time waste me;
> For now hath Time made me his numb'ring clock.
> My thoughts are minutes, and with sighs they jar
> Their watches on unto mine eyes, the outward watch,
> Whereto my finger, like a dial's point,
> Is pointing still, in cleansing them from tears.
> Now, sir, the sound that tells what hour it is
> Are clamorous groans which strike upon my heart,
> Which is the bell. So sighs, and tears, and groans
> Show minutes, times, and hours. But my time
> Runs posting on in Bolingbroke's proud joy,
> While I stand fooling here, his jack o'the clock. (*Richard II*, 5.5. 49–60)

Richard's sighs become the mechanical indicators of time passing, shocking the body by materialising his inward thoughts every minute, projecting or ejecting them ("jar their watches unto mine eyes") to the outside.[56] Examining sighs translates into ordering disordered breathing, but this process is communicated as knowledge of loss. Forcefully expelled from the body, and registering the body's resignation, sighing can be seen to embody death, as Brandon LaBelle has argued exploring the "oral imaginary" or else the ways that the mouth gestures: "the sigh" he writes, "is a sort of rehearsal of one's dying moment: it shadows the body's ultimate gasp, that final sound and respiration."[57] Emptying the body the moment they are expelled, sighs can only be experienced as loss. As a result, writing of suspiration and attempting to capture it, or better recapture it, ultimately succumb to a type of representation whereby loss of air can only be accounted for by attempts to repossess it.

Representation evaporates. In a speech shortly before he dies, Hamlet's final plea with Horatio is for an orchestrated sigh, one that is produced pathologically in pain but turns into wasted air into the play we see in front of us:

> HAMLET: As thou'rt a man
> Give me the cup. Let go. By heaven, I'll have't.
> O God, Horatio, what a wounded name,
> Things standing thus unknown, shall I leave behind me!
> If thou didst ever hold me in thy heart,
> Absent thee from felicity awhile,
> And in this harsh world draw thy breath in pain,
> To tell my story. (5.2. 327–33)

This scene is usually delivered with Hamlet dying in Horatio's hands, sighing often and heavily due to the physical exhaustion of the duel with Laertes and the fact he has been wounded by him with a poisoned sword. In most productions, Hamlet's exhaustion is accentuated after physically struggling to stop Horatio from committing suicide either by shouting, running over to him or even wrestling for the cup. Knowing these are Hamlet's final moments, we as the audience are invited to pay close attention to every word he speaks, perhaps—depending on seating arrangements—suspending our breathing patterns to catch his last words, and what is hard to ignore is the prince's heavy breathing, in some cases coupled with Horatio's heavy breathing, the sighs of both locked and exchanged between them. Actors and audience are breathing together and are short of air at the same time, a shared emotional and suffocating experience. Sale has argued that Hamlet asks to breathe through Horatio who will communicate his breath to the audience, but my understanding is that Hamlet in asking Horatio to "draw his breath in pain" is asking him specifically to sigh.[58] Sighing in this respect is called upon to assume the role of storytelling, of representing, of constructing narratives out of one's private experience and of ordering what has been in disorder—all of which sighs are perceived to do. And yet, considering the temporality of each theatrical production that reorders, rehearses, repeats and re-enacts, *Hamlet* epitomises the slippery significations of sighing and the experience of loss inherent in all representation. This loss is always inevitable but never absolute in the world of the theatre and in the world of Hamlet. Having witnessed Hamlet's evaporating final breath and its channelling through Horatio onto the atmosphere of the playhouse, our emotions work to sustain the illusion of Hamlet's dead body and to overlook the actor's now quiet rhythmical movement of the chest. As Carol Rutter writes with regard to Cordelia's corpse, "speechless, motionless, reduced by death from somebody to the body, the corpse, the actor's body occupies a theatrical space of pure performance where it has most to play when it has least to act. It is a subject-made-object whose presence registers absence and loss."[59] What refuses the transition from subject to object is breath, the unmistakable sign of life outside the control of any actor, that restores the dead body of the character to its vitality even after it has exhaled its dying groan.

But Hamlet's dying groan refuses to be a sign of death. In its indeterminacy and visible invisibility, his last gasp of air is neither his last nor a gasp but exceeds both, as it revitalises matter and eludes representation.

The "O, O, O, O" line that appears in the First Folio after Hamlet's words "The rest is silence" (5.2. 342) is not found in the second quarto and has allowed for scholarly speculation by editors and critics. Hibbard, in his Oxford edition, chooses to replace the line with the stage direction "he gives a long sigh and dies," whereas the Arden editors, faithful to the second quarto, relegate the four Os to the footnotes and call them "a conventional indication of a dying groan or sigh." Investigating stage history, Tiffany Stern has suggested that the line found in the Folio but not in the good quarto might have been added by the Shakespearean actor, Richard Burbage:

> could it be that Burbage, playing Hamlet, wanted a more glamorous death-scene than the one the text gave him? As it appears, Burbage has frustrated the wishes of the author for a reflective, silent death, by imposing on to his part a noisily vocal death-rattle, though it ruins the tenor of the last lines.[60]

Stern assigns multiple meanings to the sigh: it is an extravagant indication of death, it is loud and noisy, it is disrespectful to the silent, sacred death scene Shakespeare intended, and it is symptomatic of an actor's virtuosic performance and an opportunity for them to elide authorial control. When juxtaposed with an actor's perspective, however, and experience of delivering the elusive line, editorial interventions to pin down its meaning can be seen as part of an apparatus that measures and delineates but remains detached from the phenomenon of sighing that unfolds on stage. In a 2009 radio interview, Mark Rylance was asked to comment on whether these four sounds represent "a nothingness or something."[61] Sighing audibly and on cue before offering his answer, Rylance struggled to explain away the sighs he enacted. After deliberation and pausing often, his response was that the "O, O, O, O" is the moment (or the four distinct moments) of "encountering another reality than was immediate apparent to those around me"[62] but one that cannot be captured in words: "his [Hamlet's] ability to put words to what he's witnessing dies before his ability to witness."[63] In place of the narrative that breaks down, the sigh's energy explodes in unpredictable material directions: on some occasions, Rylance would deliver the line "silently, looking four times in four different places," or he would "change tempo," but he admits that the "best deaths" occurred on nights "when audience and I were together" aware that "something is happening but we do not know what it is, then he [Hamlet] is gone."⁶⁴ Including the line in the text is giving air a boundary, circumscribing it, describing it, representing it, closing it down and measuring it, yet on stage, on radio and in life the Os of a sigh are constantly expelled, absorbed, having no boundaries.

Notes

1. Not all editors agree with the excision; Thompson and Taylor have retained this passage for the Arden. Hibbard's glosses of lines 4.7.112–121 appear in the Appendix A in the Oxford edition (2008), which is the edition this essay refers to when citing from *Hamlet*.
2. *Hamlet*, 367.
3. Walsh (1997, 173).
4. See Malone (1821, 454–456).
5. For a full discussion of editorial proceedings of this line and passage, see Walsh 173–174.
6. Bacon (1627, 184).
7. Katie Barclay, for instance, has made this case for historians of emotions: "relationships, networks, histories become 'matter', while leaving matter behind or unidentified." Barclay (2017, 179).
8. Barad (2007, 137).
9. *OED* online: to bear, convey or remove from one person, place or condition to another; to transfer, transport.
10. Barad (2007, 137).
11. Ibid., 150.
12. For the distinction between objects/objectivity (traditionally seen as having exterior, separate and clearly defined material boundaries) and phenomena (open-ended practices of reconfiguration that characterise intra-action), see Barad, chapter 3, esp. 146–175. As Barad states in her introduction, "phenomena do not merely mark the epistemological inseparability of observer and observed, or the results of measurements (in other words, objects); rather, *phenomena* are the *ontological* inseparability of agentially intra-acting components. Significantly, phenomena are not mere laboratory creations but basic units of reality" (33, Barad's emphasis).
13. Sale (2006, 157).
14. Mazzio (2009, 169–170).
15. Ibid., 154.
16. Ibid., 148.
17. Coole and Frost (2010, 8).
18. Bennett (2010, ix).

19. *OED* online.
20. Ibid.
21. See West (2014); for an admittedly brief discussion of respiration in the Renaissance, see Lindeman (1999); for a detailed history, see Murray Kinsman (1927).
22. Quoted in West (2014, L122).
23. Aristotle, transl. by W.S. Hett (1936, XX, 479b, 17-XXI, 480b, 12).
24. Debru (2015, 273).
25. Alexander of Aphrodisias (1595, XXII, K4).
26. Wright (1604, 61).
27. Bright (1586, 158).
28. Coeffetaeu (1621, 171–172).
29. Ferrand (1640, 133).
30. Bright, 161, and Coeffetaeu, 273.
31. Ramirez (2014, 17).
32. Radford (2016); see also Krasnow and Feldman (2016).
33. Li and Yackle (2017, R89).
34. Vlemincx et al. (2010a, 86).
35. Ibid., 86.
36. Vlemincx et al. "Take a Deep Breath" (2010b, 72); see also Vlemincx et al. (2015, 664–665).
37. Ibid., 72.
38. Bright (1586, 161).
39. Vlemincx et al. "Take a Deep Breath" (2010b, 68).
40. Whitehead and Woods (2016, 7).
41. Barad makes the distinction between objects and phenomena in her study.
42. Li and Yackle (2017, R89).
43. Ibid., R89.
44. Ramirez (2014, 3).
45. Ibid., 17.
46. "The idea of the medical humanities having a 'role' to play within a wider research ecology presupposes the sanitary division of disciplines rather than the messy and mixed hybridities, collaborations and dilutions that underpin much of its work" (Viney et al. 2015, 4).
47. Ramirez (2014, 3).
48. Barclay (2017, 180). The bodily experience of emotions has been the subject of multiple studies on early modern literature and drama (including Shakespeare) since the turn of the century. The materialism of new historicist readings of the passions in the renaissance, despite its influential challenge to the dualistic boundaries of Pauline theology and to symbolic interpretations of the body, has itself been on the receiving end of criticism. Richard Strier, for instance, has reacted to the work

of Gail Kern Paster and Michael C. Schoenfeldt for what he sees as an insistence on using humoral theory as the master-discourse of the period and in effect pathologising the subject, privileging the embodied interiority of passions (see, for instance, Paster 2004; Paster et al. 2004; and Schoenfeldt 1999). According to Strier, the "new humoralism" of this critical school "produces readings that are extraordinarily and consistently conservative, readings that entirely support the rule of order, reason, and restraint" (17–18). Robert S. White and Ciara Rawnsley recently remind us that "specific circumstances and affective responses become more complex than such an approach can accommodate" (241). The revisionary tendencies of renaissance scholarship articulated in the last decade have emerged in the context of wider scepticism about the "affective turn," or else about the movement in neurosciences, psychology and philosophy that developed in the turn of our century with thinkers like Antonio Damasio, and their influence on figures, such as Brian Massumi, who focused on the body's autonomous capacity to respond, interact and feel prior to the brain's application of any cognitive interpretative strategies. Yet, as Ruth Leys argues, the validation of the body as the pure, pre-conscious, determinant has come at the expense of endowing its experiences with any meaning: "what we are witnessing today is the embrace by the new affect theorists in the humanities and social sciences of the same anti-intentionalism that for more than twenty years now has been entrenched in the sciences of affect" (469).

49. See Mullaney (2007, 74).
50. Quoted in Scheer (2012, 201).
51. Scheer (2012, 201–202), see also Reddy (2001), Rosenwein (2006), and Plamper (2010).
52. Ibid., 201–202.
53. Ibid., 207.
54. Ibid., 219.
55. There's again a point to be made here about the use and the limits of narrative in medical humanities, as advocated by Angela Woods (2011).
56. See Shakespeare, *King Richard II* (2002).
57. LaBelle (2014, 85).
58. Sale (2006, 161–162).
59. Rutter (2001, 2).
60. Stern (2004, 89).
61. Rylance (2009, min 5, sec 30–38).
62. Ibid., min 6, sec 10–30.
63. Ibid., min 6, sec 40–46.
64. Ibid., min 7, sec 1–35.

References

Alexander of Aphrodisias (although Aristotle is listed as the author). 1595. *Physitians*. Edinburgh: Printed by Robert Waldgrave.

Aristotle. 1936. *On Respiration*, trans. W.S. Hett. The Loeb Classical Library. Cambridge: Harvard University Press.

Bacon, Francis. 1627. *Sylva Sylvarum: Or, A Natural History in Ten Centuries*. London: Printed for W. Lee.

Barad, Karen. 2007. *Meeting the Universe Halfway: Quantum Physics and the Entanglement of Matter and Meaning*. Durham: Duke University Press.

Barclay, Katie. 2017. New Materialism and the New History of Emotions. *Emotions: History Culture, Society* 1: 161–183.

Bennett, Jane. 2010. *Vibrant Matter: A Political Ecology of Things*. Durham: Duke University Press.

"bowel." *OED* Online. Oxford: University Press. www.oed.com. Accessed 26 Apr 2018.

Bright, Timothy. 1586. *A Treatise of Melancholie*. London: Printed by Thomas Vautrollier.

Coeffeteau, Nicolas. 1621. *A Table of Humane Passions with Their Causes and Effects*. London: Printed by Nicholas Okes.

Coole, Diana H., and Samantha Frost (eds.). 2010. *New Materialisms: Ontology, Agency, and Politics*. Durham: Duke University Press.

Debru, Armelle. 2015. Physiology. In *The Cambridge Companion to Galen*, ed. R.J. Hankinson, 263–282. Cambridge: Cambridge University Press.

Ferrand, Jacques. 1640. *Erotomania: Or, A Treatise Discoursing of the Essence, Causes, Symptomes, Prognosticks, and Cure of Love, or Erotique Melancholy*. Oxford: Printed by L. Lichfield.

Krasnow, Mark A., and Jack L. Feldman. 2016. The Peptidergic Control Circuit for Sighing. *Nature* 530: 293–297.

LaBelle, Brandon. 2014. *Lexicon of the Mouth: Poetics and Politics of Voice and the Oral Imaginary*. London: Bloomsbury.

Leys, Ruth. 2011. The Turn to Affect: A Critique. *Critical Inquiry* 37: 434–472.

Li, Peng, and Kevin Yackle. 2017. Sighing. *Current Biology* 27: R83–R102.

Lindemann, Mary. 1999. *Medicine and Society in Early Modern Europe*. Cambridge: Cambridge University Press.

Malone, Edmond (ed.). 1821. *The Plays and Poems of William Shakespeare*, vol. III. London: Printed for F.C. and J. Rivington et al.

Mazzio, Carla. 2009. The History of Air: *Hamlet* and the Trouble with Instruments. *South Central Review* 26: 153–196.

Mullaney, Steven. 2007. Affective Technologies: Toward an Emotional Logic of the Elizabethan Stage. In *Environment and Embodiment in Early Modern*

England, ed. Mary Floyd-Wilson and Garrett A. Sullivan, 71–89. Basingstoke: Palgrave Macmillan.
Murray Kinsman, J. 1927. The History of the Study of Respiration. Presented to the Innominate Society. http://innominatesociety.com/Articles/The%20 History%20of%20the%20Study%20of%20Respiration.htm. Accessed 27 Apr 2018.
Paster, Gail Kern. 2004. *Humoring the Body: Emotions and the Shakespeare Stage*. Chicago: University of Chicago Press.
Paster, Gail Kern, Katherine Rowe, and Mary Floyd-Wilson (eds.). 2004. *Reading the Early Modern Passions: Essays in the Cultural History of Emotion*. Philadelphia: University of Pennsylvania Press.
Plamper, Jan. 2010. The History of Emotions: An Interview with William Reddy, Barbara Rosenwein, and Peter Stearns. *History and Theory* 49: 237–265.
Radford, Tim. 2016. A Sigh Is Not Just a Sigh—It's a Fundamental Life-Sustaining Reflex. *The Guardian*, February 8.
Ramirez, Jan-Marino. 2014. The Integrative Role of the Sigh in Psychology, Physiology, Pathology, and Neurobiology. *Progress in Brain Research* 209: 91–129.
Reddy, William. 2001. *The Navigation of Feeling: Framework for the History of Emotions*. Cambridge: Cambridge University Press.
Rosenwein, Barbara H. 2006. *Emotional Communities in the Early Middle Ages*. Ithaca: Cornell University Press.
Rutter, Carol Chillington. 2001. *Enter the Body: Women and Representation on Shakespeare's Stage*. London and New York: Routledge.
Rylance, Mark. 2009. Radiolab Blog. No. 14: The Four Groans. WNYC. The interview with Rylance starts at min 3, sec 20. http://bufvc.ac.uk/shakespeare/index.php/title/av73669. Accessed 8 Jan 2018.
Sale, Carolyn. 2006. Eating Air, Feeling Smells: *Hamlet*'s Theory of Performance. *Renaissance Drama* 35: 145–168.
Scheer, Monique. 2012. Are Emotions a Kind of Practice (and is That What Makes Them Have a History)? A Bourdieuian Approach to Understanding Emotion. *History and Theory* 51 (2): 193–220.
Schoenfeldt, Michael C. 1999. *Bodies and Selves in Early Modern England: Physiology and Inwardness in Spenser, Shakespeare, Herbert, and Milton*. Cambridge: Cambridge University Press.
Shakespeare, William. 1987, reissued 2008. *Hamlet*, ed. G.R. Hibbard. Oxford: Oxford University Press.
Shakespeare, William. 2002. *King Richard II*, ed. Charles R. Forker. London: Bloomsbury.
Shakespeare, William. 2006. *Hamlet*, ed. Ann Thompson and Neil Taylor. London: Bloomsbury.

Stern, Tiffany. 2004. *Making Shakespeare: From Stage to Page*. London and New York: Routledge.
Strier, Richard. 2011. *The Unrepentant Renaissance: From Petrarch to Shakespeare to Milton*. Chicago: University of Chicago Press.
"suspiration." *OED* Online. Oxford: University Press. www.oed.com. Accessed 26 Apr 2018.
"transfer." *OED* Online. Oxford University Press. www.oed.com. Accessed 27 Apr 2018.
Viney, William, Felicity Callard, and Angela Woods. 2015. Critical Medical Humanities: Embracing Entanglement, Taking Risks. *Medical Humanities* 41: 2–7.
Vlemincx, Elke, et al. 2010a. Respiratory Variability Preceding and Following Sighs: A Resetter Hypothesis. *Biological Psychology* 84: 82–87.
Vlemincx, Elke, et al. 2010b. Take a Deep Breath: The Relief Effect of Spontaneous and Instructed Sighs. *Physiology & Behavior* 101: 62–73.
Vlemincx, Elke, Ilse Van Diest, and Omer Van den Bergh. 2015. Emotion, Sighing, and Respiratory Variability. *Psychophysiology* 52: 657–666.
Walsh, Marcus. 1997. *Shakespeare, Milton and the Eighteenth-Century Literary Editing*. Cambridge: Cambridge University Press.
West, John. 2014. Galen and the Beginnings of Western Physiology. *American Journal of Physiology—Lung Cellular and Molecular Physiology* 307: L121–L128.
White, Robert S., and Ciara Rawnsley. 2015. Discrepant Emotional Awareness in Shakespeare. In *The Renaissance of Emotion: Understanding Affect in Shakespeare and His Contemporaries*, ed. Richard Meek and Erin Sullivan, 241–263. Manchester: Manchester University Press.
Whitehead, Anne, and Angela Woods. 2016. Introduction. In *The Edinburgh Companion to the Critical Medical Humanities*, ed. Anne Whitehead et al., 1–31. Edinburgh: Edinburgh University Press.
Woods, Angela. 2011. The Limits of Narrative: Provocations for the Medical Humanities. *Medical Humanities* 37: 73–78.
Wright, Thomas. 1604. *The Passions of the Minde in General*. London: Printed by Valentine Simmes and Adam Islip.

Open Access This chapter is licensed under the terms of the Creative Commons Attribution 4.0 International License (http://creativecommons.org/licenses/by/4.0/), which permits use, sharing, adaptation, distribution and reproduction in any medium or format, as long as you give appropriate credit to the original author(s) and the source, provide a link to the Creative Commons license and indicate if changes were made.

The images or other third party material in this chapter are included in the chapter's Creative Commons license, unless indicated otherwise in a credit line to the material. If material is not included in the chapter's Creative Commons license and your intended use is not permitted by statutory regulation or exceeds the permitted use, you will need to obtain permission directly from the copyright holder.

CHAPTER 4

Out of Breath: Respiratory Aesthetics from Ruskin to Vernon Lee

Peter Garratt

Abstract This chapter examines the roles played by respiration—as physiological process, and embodied response—in the development of aesthetic theories at the end of the nineteenth century, traced from Ruskin to Vernon Lee. Late nineteenth-century attempts to define aesthetic experience in terms of its attendant physiological reactions still drew on breath's immaterial poetic associations (air, wind and spirit) while being alert to the way respiratory control shifts easily between voluntary and involuntary modes of experience (will/automation). Lee's idea of aesthetic experience envisages a complex, perhaps mystifying, action of involvement with works of art, dependent upon physiological, sensorimotor and respiratory movement. Exploring her understanding of empathetic identification, and relating it to current models of enactive cognition, the chapter recovers an entangled art and science of breath in nineteenth-century aesthetic theory.

Keywords Breath · Aesthetics · Affect · Physiology · Psychology · Empathy · Enactivism

Let me begin with three markings of breath:

> Abundant images no more make a poem than any number of swallows make a summer. ... True poetry is as real, as needful, and naturally as common to every man as the blood of his heart and the breath of his nostrils.
> (E. S. Dallas, *Poetics: An Essay on Poetry*, 1852)[1]

> The sea-beach round this isle of ours is the frieze of our Parthenon, every wave that breaks on it thunders with Athena's voice; nay, whenever you throw your window wide open in the morning, you let in Athena, as wisdom and fresh air at the same instant; and whenever you draw a pure, long, full breath of right heaven, you take Athena into your heart, through your blood; and with the blood, into the thoughts of your brain.
> (John Ruskin, *The Queen of the Air*, 1869)[2]

> If experience consists of impressions, it may be said that impressions *are* experience, just as (have we not seen it?) they are the very air we breathe.
> (Henry James, "The Art of Fiction," 1884)[3]

Breath, usually so hard to see or notice, receives here three different encodings in the language of nineteenth-century aesthetics, each one disclosing an intimacy between art and the action of breathing that surpasses the purely figurative.[4] In the first, by the scientific literary critic E. S. Dallas, whose mid-century *Poetics* channelled the deductive reasoning of Aristotle and Bacon, and also in the third, by Henry James, respiration is used as a sign of naturalness that establishes the imbrication of art in life. In the Dallas and James passages, poetry and aesthetic experience (under the rubric of the "impression") emerge not merely as *analogues* of physiological vitality but as modes of its extension or unfolding. Art, in the broadest sense, aligns with the lived world, partaking of and flourishing within its atmosphere (atmosphere being another pointedly Jamesian term in "The Art of Fiction").[5] If both wish, in different ways, to naturalise the domain of aesthetics by aligning it with organic rhythms of reciprocation, of which breathing is an exemplary case, then this is organised into two distinct emphases. One of these falls on the significance of nonconscious or reflex action. Notice how insistently Dallas, for one, subordinates poetic image to poetic form, for what embeds "true poetry" in the lived or natural order is not its power of semantic reference—not imagery or theme or other devices of denotation—but the fact of its rhythm and continuity, its way of pushing on, in sympathy with the persistence of breath. A second emphasis, also on living process, connects breath with consciousness by asserting that impressions (of art and of life) are a kind of oxygenation (James). But in the Ruskin passage, contrastingly, one finds no such naturalisation. Beguilingly, in *The Queen of the Air*, more or less the reverse holds: Ruskin locates Greek myth in the circulating air, and in the body's essential strivings and chemical transformations, as though the goddess Athena might literally be assimilated by the tissues. Ordinary breath, usually beneath awareness, now feels ontologically lithe, a shaping force composed of air, myth and matter, connecting the lungs with a vast transpersonal system of circulation and meaning. Ruskin's breath, then, is exultantly defamiliarised, converting an invisible substance into an aesthetically visible and vital one.

In this chapter, I want to trace the development of these subtle tensions and topoi, as a way of understanding breath and breathing in the progressively materialist aesthetics of the late nineteenth century. Styling this as "respiratory aesthetics" is more than a convenience, I hope, and intends to bring into focus the special importance of breath to debates over the province of art, and art's genesis, form and force, as the late-Victorian moment shades into early modernist culture, particularly in the critical thought of Vernon Lee (Violet Paget). The questions I seek to address through Lee—of how and why certain ideas of breath and breathing come to bear upon theories of aesthetic form by the end of the nineteenth century, of how breath matters to the experience of art—relate to a larger field of enquiry, loosely identified as Victorian scientific aesthetics, which has already been influentially mapped by Nicholas Dames and, recently, Benjamin Morgan.[6] Shifting down an analytical level, such questions also contain narrower subsets, including how understandings of the physiology of respiration influenced nineteenth-century prosody, a topic explored lucidly by Jason Rudy and Jason Hall.[7] If neither the higher nor the lower level is the target of my argument, what I hope to recover through Vernon Lee and other theoreticians, from Ruskin and Dallas onwards, has much in common with these critics' interest in a Victorian turn to physiological systems for an explanation of art's embodied life.

As a writer and intellectual who straddled literary periods and cut across the diverging "two cultures" of art and science, Lee helps to illuminate particular ways in which breathing gathered meanings within British aesthetic tradition in the era roughly between the highpoint of Ruskin's influence and the 1920s. Prolific as a novelist, critic, essayist, art historian and author of supernatural stories, as well as an aesthetician, she had a close association with Walter Pater and aestheticism, embraced decadence and impressionism, subsequently absorbed Nietzsche's philosophy of tragedy, and in politics held committedly socialist, pacifist and feminist views.[8] At the same time, she drew on, extended and challenged the scientific naturalism of Darwin and mid-Victorian psychology (Alexander Bain, Herbert Spencer), while engaging closely with contemporary German thought, notably the psychology of Theodore Lipps, leading Lee to apply empirical and statistical methods to the study of art.[9] In other words, various influences flow into, and through, her critical prose and mingle in its expository textures. Those emphases that organise the breathy passages above—on reflex action (Dallas), vitality/flow (Ruskin) and embodied thought (James)—can all be discovered in Lee's writings on visual art, music, and language and literature. Recovering breath's substance and freight in these works may seem to confirm Lee's intellectual singularity, as I say, but it has the further advantage of making visible a wider history of respiratory aesthetics that belongs to late-Victorian modernity.

Art Unthought

In "Ruskinism" (1881), her forthright early work of intellectual self-positioning, Vernon Lee magnificently dismantles Ruskin's preachy excesses on the morality of art. Everywhere, she complains, Ruskin equates the good with the beautiful—a fundamental, erroneous conflation, ripe for renunciation—because of a residual puritanism in Ruskin that cannot admit aesthetic pleasure on its own terms and must instead annex it to some higher purpose. Ruskin's whole ethics of criticism comes down to this point: the sensuous wellsprings of beauty remain troublingly diverting, and in need of moral and spiritual rescue, such that sinful gratification must be converted into noblest virtue. "Ruskin has loved art instinctively, fervently, for its own sake," Lee points out, admiringly, "but he has constantly feared lest this love should be sinful or at least base."[10] In consequence, he "must tranquillize his conscience about art; he must persuade himself that he is justified in employing his thoughts about it; and lest it be a snare of the demon, he must make it a service of God."[11] At root, as revealed in his most characteristic moments, Ruskin "made the enjoyment of mere beauty a base pleasure, requiring a moral object to purify it, and in so doing he has destroyed its own purifying power."[12]

As "Ruskinism" ends, with Lee now eased into the aesthete's role, the essay yields an affirmation of startling dexterity, in its own way a kind of inverted Ruskinism, which celebrates pleasure's intrinsic virtue: "For, though art has no moral meaning, it has a moral value; art is happiness, and to bestow happiness is to create good."[13] This is hedonist aesthetics housed in the stately precincts of Victorian high seriousness.

What emerges from Lee's effort to displace Ruskin—and what matters from the perspective of breath—is an accompanying return to less conceptual and more instinctual modes of relational awareness anchored in the body. When Lee announces in her introduction to *Belcaro* (1881), the book in which "Ruskinism" appeared, that her purpose in discussing art will be to re-engage a mood of childish enjoyment, she describes turning her back decisively on once cherished texts of high aesthetic theory—her well-thumbed and carefully annotated Plato and Hegel, her Ruskin and Taine—in order to establish the possibility of a direct encounter with works of art. Such a gesture of uncluttering ("getting rid of those foreign, extra-artistic, irrelevant interests which aestheticians have since the beginning of time interposed between art and those who are intended to enjoy it") clears a path for what will become her distinctive approach to understanding objects displayed in galleries, music and poetry, even when less overtly sympathetic to the ideas of the Aesthetic Movement.[14] In *Belcaro*, she recalls discovering the poverty of theory as a primal recognition:

> Much as I read, copied, annotated, analysed, imitated [these authorities], I could not really take in any of the things which I read .... As soon as I got back in the presence of art itself, all my carefully acquired artistic philosophy, mystic, romantic, or transcendental, was forgotten: I looked at pictures and statues, and saw in them mere lines and colours, pleasant or unpleasant; I listened to music, and ... I discovered that, during the period of listening, my mind had been a complete blank, and that all I could possibly recollect were notes. My old original prosaic, matter-of-fact feeling about art, as something simple, straightforward, enjoyable, always persisted beneath all the metaphysics and all the lyrism with which I tried to crush it.[15]

Rediscovering the "presence" of art is, in one sense, an abiding purpose in each of *Belcaro*'s layered, meandering essays, and the term surfaces insistently here amidst a crystalline memory of responding to some artistic patterns and forms ("mere" lines and colours, pure sequences of musical notes) with a felt sense of involvement, yet little, if any, accompanying representational awareness. Music, in the moment, was a "blank"; pictures and sculptures were enjoyable purely as objects comprised of structured visual elements.

Art's real mode of presence, this suggests, comes before its emergence as an object of knowledge. Preceding categories of knowledge and judgment, its presence is both pre-ethical and grounded on an impressionable yet preconscious body, the body of its percipient subject. As this begins to indicate, art's way of being present can be framed in terms of *action*, a point emphasised throughout Lee's writing on aesthetics, right up to her last published work, *Music and Its Lovers* (1932), where she describes the artwork as a "junction between the activities of the artist and those of the beholder or hearer."[16] Far from signalling the contemplation of an ineffable object whose nature remains wordlessly withdrawn, or pointing towards modernism's austere poetics of impersonality, presence (understood as action) registers something like a feat of coordination, perhaps better parsed as co-presence or interaction—that is to say, the embodied co-presence of, on the one hand, a beholder, listener or reader and, on the other, a canvas, sonata or poem (say), extended together in time. Put like this, aesthetic experience has discernable features: the quality of duration, the structure of dynamic coupling or interaction, and it constitutes a form of doing.

In outline, Lee's quarrel with Ruskinism was roughly of a piece with Walter Pater's inwardly focused "first step" of aesthetic criticism: the creed of knowing one's own impressions rather than seeking to know the art object in itself.[17] In common with post-Paterian British literary decadence, Lee accorded special importance to the notion of impressionability. The mind of the critic, now exemplary, was defined by how appropriately susceptible it could prove itself. What power does an artwork have to affect me? How does it elicit my impressions of beauty or pleasure? By making fleeting personal impressions the decisive locus of value, instead of treating high art as the intrinsic material instantiation of abstract ideals, as the moralists Ruskin and Arnold had done, late-Victorian critics channelled the "relative spirit" of the final quarter of the century.[18] As Daniel Hannah puts it, "[t]he Paterian impression and Wilde's and [Henry] James's adaptations of it shift the focus of aesthetic analysis from the text as embodied meaning to the critic as ecstatic artist."[19] The same went for Lee, in general terms. But, at a more exacting level of scrutiny, it is clear that she diverged from Paterian subjectivism, in key respects. If the subject of impressionism risked being marooned in a swirl of fleeting, wispy appearances (i.e. to say, in the realm of mental representation), as Pater had hinted at in his infamous "Conclusion" to *Studies in the History of the Renaissance*,[20] then Lee's interest after *Belcaro* was increasingly taken up with the role of the responsive body in aesthetic cognition, including sensorimotor movements, reflex actions and the bodily unconscious.[21] One focus of her later empirical investigations was the background arousal, the affective to-and-fro, of breathing, as I discuss later on. Pre-conceptual knowing would underpin her view of how people succeed in being immersively involved with cultural objects in their proximate environment—an empathy with things seen or heard, by means of a process I am characterising as active coupling—without arriving at the brink of solipsism and disengagement.[22]

Even if Pater's psychology implicitly recognised the "corporeal mediation of thought," as Benjamin Morgan has suggested, a consequential feature of Vernon Lee's way of thinking about impressionability was its strongly physical—its physiological, its neuromuscular—character[23] Physiological impressions did not necessarily rise to introspective consciousness; she considered them part of cognitive activity, in the sense of being an unthought component of attentive perception, even if they bypassed explicit representational encoding in the mind. Automatic and reflex actions—of the sort exemplified by breathing—thereby came into the orbit of her aesthetic theory. Such an overlap can be found in other critics and writers of the late-Victorian era. We have already seen how Henry James could think of impressions as inhalations—continuous, instinctive, commonplace, like the very air we breathe. Edith Wharton, in 1903, would passingly declare (in a fascinatingly prickly essay about the state of the novel and novel-readers) that "real reading is reflex action; the born reader reads as unconsciously as he breathes."[24] As with James's decidedly exclusive appeal to a "we" who inhales impressions of life, Wharton's recourse to respiratory language conveys the opposite of something ordinary or democratic: an aristocratic sense of literacy as effortless, inborn, and inevitable, in contrast to the self-improving exertion of newly educated readers from the expanding middle classes, for whom books were all about consciously invested labour and deferred reward.

Talk of unconscious processes reached back further into the nineteenth century, however. The importance of instinctive actions to mind and body, especially perception, had been established by mid-Victorian psychology and then annexed by peripheral debates in aesthetics and scientific literary criticism, which helps explain why the phrase "reflex action" came so readily to Wharton's lips. Wharton, as one can hear, took it to mean something organic and vital, and not a name for compulsive mechanical twitchings of the flesh and muscle. If reading was reflex action, it was so because reflexes had now acceded to cognitive office. The new physiological psychology of the 1850s and 60s, in pioneering this view, had rewritten earlier mechanistic understandings of the physiological body, showing how reflex actions and unconscious processes were tied to the thought and agency of the person as a unified living organism. In fact, Darwin's "bulldog," T. H. Huxley, used nothing other than the act of reading to explain the principle of reflex action in his incredibly popular *Lessons of Elementary Physiology* (1866), alongside the example of a soldier perfecting military drill exercises at an officer's command (that being a learnt or "artificial" reflex, showing how all education might involve, at root, "organizing conscious actions into more or less unconscious, or reflex, operations").[25] When we read a book, Huxley observed, we hold it automatically at an optimal distance from our eyes, adjust our posture suitably and make countless "delicate" movements with our hands and eyes as we read, mostly without noticing that we are doing any of this.[26] A similar theory was intended by the physiologist W. B. Carpenter when, in 1854, he coined the influential phrase "unconscious cerebration," a term which can be parsed as thinking without thinking, as Vanessa Ryan has styled it.[27] For the critic E. S. Dallas, unconscious thought and actions were evidence of a "hidden reason" operating outside our awareness, "a power that with the greatest ease reaches spontaneously to results beyond reckoning, beyond understanding."[28]

Respiration was, of course, both exemplary and a special category here. If breathing offered a powerful instance of automatic reflex action—as Dallas put it, "the brain keeps guard over the various processes of the body—as the beating of the heart and the breathing of the lungs"—then it had the further characteristic of being able to flit between involuntary regulation and temporary volitional control.[29] In this respect, argued George Henry Lewes, the influential man of science and Victorian polymath, respiration had something in common with phenomena like winking and laughter, which in some situations cannot be prevented from occurring, however hard we actively resist, while at other times they obey the influence of the conscious will (as in winking to signal ironic intent, or laughing politely at an unfunny remark). A sneeze, which cannot be willed, would be an example of a purely involuntary action. Breathing, then, dramatised for Lewes the limits and nature of our embodied agency: "Although breathing is an involuntary act, it can be, and often is, restrained or accelerated by the will; but the controlling power soon come to an end—we cannot voluntarily suspend our breathing for many seconds; the urgency of the sensation at last bears down the control."[30] In other important ways, breathing was a deep puzzle. *Why* we breathe, as opposed to how we do so, remained unclear to science, Lewes noted. It was, patently, a matter of life and death. But why does insufficient fresh air cause death in an organism when the blood in its arteries still holds oxygen? Why does a newborn baby sometimes require external help from a doctor or nurse, who slaps them on the back, to begin to breathe?[31] "By what influence," asked the Scottish psychologist Alexander Bain, similarly, "do we draw our first breath?"[32] These were more than narrow physical enquiries to be filled out by a more detailed story of ontogeny; they concerned the will of our creaturely being and the scope of subjectivity.

They had a bearing upon aesthetic questions, too. The same hidden power that keeps the lungs expanding and contracting, day and night, and controls a host of other unnoticed vital functions, was doing the work of a "musical conductor," Dallas said.[33] This was a revealing choice of image, for Dallas was convinced that prized artistic accomplishments, such as the delicate control of a painter's brush or the compass of a soprano's voice, were made possible by the same sort of automaticity that governed breath. Conversely, the imagination was ruled only by "the sort of control which we can bring to bear on the essentially involuntary act of breathing."[34] In *The Gay Science* (1866), he marvels at the German opera singer Gertrud Mara, who had been celebrated for her unusual vocal range:

> [A]ll the 1500 varieties of musical sounds which Madame Mara could produce came from degrees in the tension of her [throat] muscles which are to be represented by dividing the eighth part of an inch into 1500 subdivisions. Which of us by taking thought can follow such arithmetic? No singer can consciously divide the tension of her vocal chords into 12,000 parts of an inch, and select one of these; nevertheless she may hit with infallible accuracy the precise note which depends upon this minute subdivision of muscular energy.[35]

Mara's artistic skill in calculating exact note intervals during an aria did not depend on explicit mental coordination, just the spontaneity of her musically trained body: a remarkable, beautiful, feat of implicit practical intelligence.

One could call it art without thinking. This was certainly Dallas's view, based on the evident conjunction of instinct and imagination, as a secret agency. Indeed, *The Gay Science* categorises some unconscious reflex actions under the term "imagination." Aesthetic and creative feelings could be fully volitional without bearing conscious effort: "The artist can trust to his hand, to his throat, to his eye, to render with unfailing accuracy subtle distinctions of tone and shades of meaning with which reason can have nothing to do – with which no effort of reason can keep pace."[36] In other words, hands or voices accomplish artistic work themselves, directly, in real time, without the mediating theatre of conscious decision-making and internal representation, just fluent sensorimotor movement. Put this way, the hypothesis invites parallels with recent enactivist cognitive science, as I shall suggest in the last section below. But a figure who Dallas invoked to corroborate his version of unconscious cerebration was none other than Ruskin: it was Ruskin, he points out, who wrote so eloquently of the "subtle instinct" of Turner's hand and its superiority over the eye when detailing very fine shades of light.[37] It was Ruskin who knew about embodied cognition.

Drawn-in Breath and Wide-Opened Eyes

While distancing herself from Ruskinism and the rhetoric of mid-Victorian criticism, Vernon Lee absorbed the influence of both. Her own respiratory aesthetics extended the then new reflex theory circulating among the likes of Lewes, Bain, Carpenter, Dallas and others, angling it towards a theory of art as experience. Ruskin himself had spoken of how great painters "do their best work without effort," by applying subtle layers of colour to a canvas in an "apparently careless" or "unconscious" fashion, yet with near-mathematical precision.[38] He included this note in an appendix to *The Two Paths* (1859), the same book in which he published "The Work of Iron, In Nature, Art and Policy," a sinuous disquisition containing a startling passage on breath:

> [W]e suppose it to be a great defect in iron that it is subject to rust. But not at all. ... Nay, in a certain sense, and almost a literal one, we may say that iron rusted is Living; but when pure or polished, Dead. ... It takes

the oxygen from the atmosphere as eagerly as we do, though it uses it differently. The iron keeps all that it gets; we, and other animals, part with it again; but the metal absolutely keeps what it has once received of this aerial gift …. [A]ll the substance of which it is made sucks and breathes the brilliancy of the atmosphere; and, as it breathes, softening from its merciless hardness, it falls into fruitful and beneficent dust; gathering itself again into the earths from which we feed, and the stones with which we build; – into the rocks that frame the mountains, and the sands that bind the sea.[39]

Originally a lecture performed to the people of Tunbridge Wells in 1858, "The Work of Iron" still quavers with the affects of live address. Here, its confounding seriousness is part of a tactic of challenging conventional formations of value: aesthetic, economic and environmental. But underneath its outwardly bizarre moralism, which insists on the nobility of rust and the beauty of decay, Ruskin unfolds a vision of distributed material vitality built around the wondrous ubiquity of oxygenation. Ironwork "breathes" and corrodes, its "dust" replenishing the earth and literally colouring the landscape (the streaks of colour in a pebble, the "violet veinings" of Sicilian marble, the purple warmth of Welsh slate), and also flowing into the human body and lending the blood its crimson: "Is it not strange to find this stern and strong metal mingled so delicately in our human life that we cannot even blush without its help?"[40] All of this derives from the world's unconscious breathwork.

In a still wholly humanist way, breath unites us with the non-human, for Ruskin: the living air affords connection, interaction, inter-existence, an idea later emblemised by Athena in *The Queen of the Air* (1869). Whatever else he means by it, breath becomes a basis for feelings of identification with the contingent life of things, and in this sense, it exercises an aesthetic potential. Grasping why intricate vermillion streaks of iron oxide running through a stone are somehow distantly connected to our living bodies—to the physiological energy that beats its rhythm in our veins and lungs—is a very particular kind of aesthetic knowing. It entails an apprehension of form as living and relational, grounded on an affective body. Now, Ruskin, always at once a paradoxically central and eccentric figure in Victorian intellectual culture, did not share obvious affinities with the likes of Bain, Carpenter or Dallas, who were among the leading the scientific lights here (though Dallas remained an admirer his *Modern Painters*).[41] He would, in fact, on occasion, parody those who aspired to explain art or beauty scientifically.[42] But one way of thinking about Ruskin's living air is to compare it, albeit counter-intuitively, with the concept of aesthetic empathy that emerged in the decadent twilight of Victorian modernity, chiefly through the collaborative investigations of Lee and her lover Clementina Anstruther-Thomson, who took their bearings from earlier materialist aesthetics and versions of unconscious cerebration as much as from Paterian idealism.

Empathy (*Einfühlung*) was not a word Ruskin used or knew, of course. Nonetheless, its sense of "feeling-into," as Vernon Lee would come to think of it, after the German philosopher Robert Vischer, captures something of Ruskin's sense of the vital attunement of subject and object that he identified with the flow of breathable air. One might notice it, too, in his example of the graceful prospect of a songbird in flight, in *The Queen of the Air*, where the bird "rests upon the air, subdues it, surpasses it, outraces it; – *is* the air, conscious of itself, conquering itself, ruling itself," and where "into the throat of the bird is given the voice of the air"—a resplendent synchrony.[43] Bird and air are ideally attuned, smoothly reciprocating, almost coalescent forces. Empathy, or in-feeling, if more specific, was an explanation of attunement. Lee imported the term in her book *The Beautiful* (1913), where she began by stating that it was a "tendency to merge the activities of the perceiving subject with the qualities of the perceived object."[44] Affective investment, as John Frow points out, had been intrinsic to theories of fictional character long before empathy's ostensible birth, and not simply in the form of obvious readerly "identification" in such narrative genres as the *Bildungsroman*.[45] Lee, too, thought the "apparent recent discovery" of empathy was only the uncanny recognition of something deeply familiar.[46] What she did *not* mean by it, however, was the sense of feeling oneself into things, the romantic-idealist identification of the self with the other through conscious egoic projection. Empathetic "mergings," as opposed to projection, required the "momentary abeyance of all thought of an ego," a lapsing of self-awareness.[47] In this respect, empathy rekindled Ruskin's denunciation of the pathetic fallacy.[48]

When, for instance, we use a commonplace expression like *the mountain rises* to describe the outline shape of a landscape, we do not consciously anthropomorphise the inanimate mountain, transferring to it a present subjective experience of rising. Nor (usually) do we mean "rising" to refer to the massive upward geological pressure that originally caused the mountain to form. The action of rising, if not strictly an objective property of its shape, is also more than just a thought prompted in us by the mountain: it is rising per se, a generalised conception of what it is to rise (the infinitive form of the verb, unconstrained by a particular tense or pronoun). Innumerable memories of lifting and raising—in ourselves (of our eyes and head, of our separate muscles and limbs and of our whole body) and experiences of it in other bodies—have fused with anticipations of such movements in the future, to form this infinitive conceptualisation of the action of rising, now separate from ourselves and the immediate unfurling of our subjective agency. Thus, the rising mountain (or the slope that goes up, or the line that drops down) involves the unconscious transfer of feelings of motion, loosed from a subject, into a quality of the static object. These examples cannot be dismissed as figures of speech or staled metaphors. For Lee, empathy (*Einfühlung*) was precisely what made figures of speech possible, a psychological mechanism underpinning meaning itself. Decades before George Lakoff and Mark Johnson identified the "metaphors we live by," she saw that empathetic identification grounded what the field of cognitive linguistics now calls embodied conceptual metaphor and, as such, it was present throughout mental life, "traced in all modes of speech and thought."[49] It was, though, especially powerful for explaining aesthetic pattern and form.

Breathing—a mostly unconscious cycle of diaphragmatic contraction and relaxation—as I enter a cathedral, stand before a landscape painting or statue, read a lyric poem or savour a cantata, plays a decisive part in the integrated suite of background responses that allow me to recognise the force of these definite aesthetic forms. For Lee, the energy of—or the energy seemingly "in"—certain patterns, shapes, lines, words, sounds and rhythms has its origins in my own responsive living breath and breathing body. The mere sight of the word *beautiful*, quite apart from any object of beauty, will often cause affective arousal within the respiratory cycle, in virtue of it "carrying a vague but potent remembrance of our own bodily reaction to the emotion of admiration; nay, even eliciting an incipient rehearsal of the half-parted lips and slightly thrown-back head, the drawn-in breath and wide-opened eyes, with which we are wont to meet opportunities of aesthetic satisfaction."[50] This reveals two features of empathetic identification, as Lee thinks about it. First, empathising does not ask of art "What is it?", having nothing strictly to do with identifications inside the representational plane of works of art, such as a novel's narrative storyworld and its represented agents and viewpoints, or the treatment of a theme by a painter or sculptor (feeling moved to pity, say, by a scene of human suffering), or the imitative properties of a heard melody. Only aspects of formal structure matter: in Lee's terminology, *shape* precedes *things*. At this level, empathy might appear peculiarly indifferent to the human context of emotional expression, and consequently easy to regard as a reaction against Victorian sentimentalism. Yet it was Ruskin rather than proponents of evolutionary science (Herbert Spencer, Grant Allen) who, for Lee, had greater authority in making a link between the emergence of aesthetic preference (beauty and ugliness) and primary bodily affects (distinguishing pleasure from pain).[51]

A second feature of note in Lee's mention of an "incipient rehearsal of … the drawn-in breath and wide-opened eyes" is that the empathetic imagination has a temporal structure of its own and tends towards revival and repetition, which Lee labels empathy's "reiterative nature."[52] Past affects remain stored in the body and contribute to habituation. Experiencing aesthetic empathy involves, at the level of the lived body, looping effects of experience, context, habituation, learning and acculturation. A tourist with limited cultural background knowledge will not respond to art objects with automatic aesthetic empathy, even before celebrated paintings or hallowed architecture.[53] This point, not without a whiff of snobbery, shows Lee resisting what she perceived to be a troubling fin de siècle tendency of translating *l'art pour l'art* into the commodification of pleasure. It also shows her resisting theories of biological essentialism: evolution has not made certain forms inherently pleasing; the mind has not been adaptively furnished with innate powers of aesthetic recognition. Instead, as a process of attunement with objects, empathy needs a personal history of embodied practice.

For these reasons, Lee's collaboration with Anstruther-Thomson in the 1880s and 90s, which led to the publication of their 1897 essay "Beauty and Ugliness" (1897), reads like a study of Clementina's visceral, muscular and respiratory life—a jointly authored memoir of the body—focusing on her experience of works of art. When reprinting "Beauty and Ugliness" in 1912, Lee announced that her evolving view of empathy was the "offspring" of its central theory.[54] Their original method of investigation, using art galleries as experimental spaces, may have appeared "kooky" and even mockable but it was taken seriously by continental psychologists and philosophers, such as Théodule Ribot and Theodor Lipps, as Caroline Burdett has shown.[55] With its almost dialogic structure, a to-and-fro of passages of each woman's writing coded by initials and typographical marks, "Beauty and Ugliness" manages to convey a kind of respiratory rhythm in its textual procedures while also fixating directly—forensically—on Clementina's breathing:

> [T]he movements of the eyes seem to have been followed by the breath. The bilateralness of the object seems to have put both lungs into play. There has been a feeling of the two sides of the chest making a sort of pull apart; the breath has begun low down and raised on both sides of the chest; a slight contraction of the chest seems to accompany the eyes as they move along the top of the chair till they got to the middle; then, when the eyes ceased focusing the chair, the breath was exhaled.[56]

One might call this physiological introspection, making the breath visible, during the process of perceiving a simple chair. These words of Anstruther-Thomson capture her, quite typically, straining to access knowledge of her own involuntary responses and actions, at the outermost edges of conscious life. This is not perceptual knowledge of an intellectual or representational kind, even if bodily mimicry may result from aesthetic empathy (e.g. unconsciously imitating the facial expression carved in a marble bust). Rather, qualities such as the chair's height, width and bulk originate in the described adjustments in the breathing apparatus and other fine motor movements. As Lee explains, "breathing and balance are the actual physical mechanism for the reception of Form, the sense of relation having for its counterpart a sense of bodily tension."[57] Our eyes and breath trace together the sweep of a rounded arch, its downward movement embodied in the unnoticed, or barely felt, exhalation of the lungs; a forward and backward motion of breath, achieved by involuntary adjustments of the thorax and diaphragm, and ordinarily present when we walk, helps with the realisation of three-dimensional depth and distance in landscape painting.[58]

Colour appreciation, the authors deduce, has a special relation to breath:

> [W]e seem *to inhale colour*. For, while stimulating the eye, we find that colour also stimulates the nostrils and the top of the throat; for a colour sensation on the eye is followed quite involuntarily by a strong movement of inspiration, producing thereby a rush of cold air through the nostrils on to the tongue and the top of the throat, and this rush of cold air has a singularly stimulating effect: sometimes the sight of an extremely vivid colour like that of tropical birds, or of vivid local colour strung up by brilliant sunshine, has a curious effect on the top of the throat, amounting to an impulse to give out a voice.[59]

Inviting their reader to experiment in various ways (holding their breath, briefly closing an eye, taking a deep lungful of air and so on), Lee and Anstruther-Thomson persist with empirical proofs of the view that "aesthetic pleasure in art is due to the production of highly vitalising, and therefore agreeable, adjustments of breathing and balance as factors of the perception of form."[60] Respiratory empathy underlies, for instance, the quality of "coolness" in Vincenzo Catena's *Saint Jerome in his Study* (1510), a painting whose colour, "by stimulating certain of our nerves connected with breathing, gives to the air which we inhale a sort of exhilarating power"; in Lee's own gallery notes, from 1904, on Raphael's frescoes in the Sistine Chapel, she reflects that "I certainly seem to see better breathing through nostrils than through mouth. The open mouth is inattention. More and more I suspect all this breathing business is a question of attention."[61] This last remark is especially suggestive: not only does it say that aesthetic form emerges out of breath, as it were, but it hints that art affords attentional interest by means of an active coupling with the body's respiratory agency.

Respiratory Aesthetics and Enactive Cognition

To flesh out this final claim in just a little more detail, let me return to the concept of presence, now engaging with it as the contemporary philosopher Alva Noë thinks about that term. Loosely, for Noë, "presence" refers to the way the world shows up for us. In visual perception, that includes more than just retinal information: the reverse side of a tomato, though not directly seen by me, is still part of my perception of the tomato; while strictly invisible, nonetheless it has presence.[62] And it has presence in virtue of my implicit knowledge that appropriate sensorimotor action (such as rotating it or moving around it) will successfully bring that invisible reverse side of the tomato into view. In *Varieties of Presence* (2012), Noë develops this approach to presence using, as it happens, the example of music:

> When you experience the singer's song, it is the singer herself, as we have noticed, that you hear. ... Perception is an action of sensorimotor coupling *with the environment*. It is not a type of engagement with mere appearances or qualia. When you attend to the sustained note, what you are thus able to establish contact with is the singer's continuous activity of holding the note. The singer and what she's doing are available to you thanks to your situation and your skillful access.[63]

Aesthetic empathy as Vernon Lee presents it similarly involves an "action of sensorimotor coupling with the environment"—though, as I will suggest in a moment, she reaches beyond Noë in an interesting way, too. Musical experience, being usefully direct and immediate for Noë, illustrates something salient about the general way all perception works on his model of enactivist cognitive science: it typically gets accomplished without mental representation ("appearances or qualia") and can instead be explained through tacit bodily knowledge. We "access" music by coupling with it, in ways that our embodied minds have learned to do. Music itself "entrains" us, in return: listening to it involves the "alignment or coordination of bodily features with recurrent features of the environment," explains another enactivist philosopher, Joel Krueger.[64] If enactivism accepts the "premise that self is embedded in world and world in self," as Katherine Hayles puts it in *Unthought* (2017), her study of the cognitive nonconscious, then one could add that this would not have sounded drastically new to proponents of Victorian psychological aesthetics.[65] For Lee, as we have seen, art achieves presence because it engages us in modes of *doing*, in sensorimotor action, not least the semi-conscious work of responsive breathing.

Music, an artistic medium especially close to the movement of breath, has a special status in Lee's writing on aesthetics, from the beginnings of her literary career. Without coincidence, her last book focused solely on music. *Music and Its Lovers* (1932) is also a methodological curiosity, given its proximity to European phenomenology, being a study of data gathered from respondents' questionnaires.[66] But already in that early volume *Belcaro* she had complained about aestheticians "not listening to the music" of pictures.[67] Her later accounts of painting and visual form retain, as Nicholas Dames has rightly noted, an insistence on music as a basic model of formal patterning in general.[68] In "Chapelmaster Kreisler," an essay in *Belcaro* (its title a reference to E. T. A. Hoffmann's fictional half-mad composer Johannes Kreisler), Lee described music as being utterly strange, its existence as sound "issuing from nothing and relapsing into nothing," at once our own human creation and yet unfathomably alien: "*it lives in our breath*, yet it seems to come from a distant land which we shall never see, and to tell us of things we shall never know."[69] In enquiring of the origins of music—and elsewhere rejecting Herbert Spencer's answer that all aesthetic activity can be traced back, in Lamarckian style, to play—Lee adopts the view that music addresses us with its sonic, yet non-semantic, force. From some impossible place, it entrains us:

> We ourselves have constant opportunities of remarking the intense emotional effects due to mere pitch, tone, and rhythm; that is to say, to the merely physical qualities of number, nature, and repetition of musical vibrations. We have all been cheered by the trumpet and depressed by the hautboy; we have felt a wistful melancholy steal over us while listening to the drone of bagpipe and the quaver of the flute of the pifferari at the shrine; *we have felt our heart beat and our breath halt* on catching the first notes of an organ as we lifted the entrance curtain of some great cathedral.[70]

In *Strange Tools* (2015), his book on art, Noë says something wholly compatible with this, if not virtually identical. Why is music enthralling? "Because," he says, "we are rhythmically and melodically and tonally organized; this is a fundamental feature of our embodied living. Music investigates these ways."[71] As for Noë, Lee's earlier version of this style of thought takes music and aesthetic experience more widely to be learned, implicit, lived practices, not prizes of evolutionary development, whether Darwinian or Spencerian, thereby enabling us to see art as something that we do.

If one suspects, in places, that Noë's enactivist account of aesthetic forms is prone to arrive at tautology—something along the lines of (though this is unfairly reductive) "art is a tool that affords art experiences"—then Lee's detailed ideas of empathetic identification might come to its aid, even perhaps adding a more nuanced and radical flavour to the sensorimotor enactivist position. For the likes of Noë and Krueger, art is an external resource, an entity with certain intrinsic qualities that we can do things with, or that afford action. To stay with the example of music, it has timbre, pitch, rhythm, variation and so forth. Krueger speaks of "sonic invariants," those "structural features of the music that specify an array of possible perceptual interactions."[72] Empathy, on the other hand, as Lee develops it, puts in question the extent to which these features are "in" the musical structure itself or rather unnoticed habitual attributions of initially unconscious bodily affects. The "fast tempo" of a musical piece is an evaluative phrase, not a value-neutral one, conventionally attributing motion to an inanimate series of individual sound units. "Fast" denotes the empathetic transfer of a primary physiological arousal, now no longer identified with the body and instead discovered as intrinsic to the music. In other words, the external acoustic structure, supposedly made up of invariants, *already* bears the imprint of interaction, one occurring at the automatic and subpersonal level of the breath and motor balance.[73]

In suggesting this, I am neither labelling Vernon Lee a sensorimotor enactivist nor staking a claim on her extraordinary prescience, both of which would be historically self-serving gestures. Pursuing Lee's relation to these present debates has value, to my mind, only to the extent that it brings into sharper focus something of her own way of thinking about art and embodiment. What this chapter has tried to do is establish the ways in which Lee's ideas of breathing and artistic creaturely flourishing established a framework of respiratory aesthetics that emerged from various sources in mid- and late-Victorian culture and yet also overspilled the containers of period boundaries, categories of art and science and different critical and artistic movements. It gave physical meaning to Walter Pater's admiring gloss of Plato: "It is not so much the *matter* of the work of art, what is conveyed in and by colour and form and sound, that tells upon us educationally … as the *form*, and its qualities, concision, simplicity, rhythm, or, contrariwise, abundance, variety, discord."[74] A sense of unconscious embodied empathy with things and persons is there in Pater's reading of Platonic mimicry, too ("we imitate unconsciously the line and colour of the walls around us").[75] Meanwhile, a language of unconscious cerebration and unfelt feelings, derived from Victorian psychology and theories of reflex action, were picked up by aesthetic debates in the 1860s and flowed on through the rhetoric of literary and critical impressionism and its decadent afterlife, as in those highlighted breathy moments in Henry James and Edith Wharton. And there was, of course, Ruskin, too. "There is, in all art," Lee affirmed as late as 1912, "what Ruskin called the Lamp of Life; and it is with it that my aesthetics deal."[76] If disentangling art from Ruskin's dubious moralism and mystification meant returning, as if pre-reflectively, to the nature of its presence, as Lee had announced in 1881, then this did not end up dispelling Ruskinism altogether. Far from it: the Ruskin who spoke of vital breath remained compatible with the world-involving action of empathy she collaboratively formulated. Like Ruskin, acculturating the instinctual will was a laudable thing. And, in broad strokes, that point locates both writers in a larger story of respiratory aesthetics at the end of the nineteenth century, a story which is now, like breath itself, only just becoming visible.

Notes

1. Dallas (1852, 270–271).
2. Ruskin (1903–1912, 19: 328–329).

3. James (1963, 86).
4. The research for this chapter came about through happy association with Durham's "Life of Breath" project, funded by the Wellcome Trust, and I wish to thank Corinne Saunders and Jane Macnaughton for inviting me to contribute to its launch event on 15 September 2015.
5. Only moments before making this connection between subjective impressions and the breath, James famously describes experience as always unlimited and incomplete, "the very atmosphere of the mind" (James 1963, 85). This section of "The Art of Fiction" flits suggestively between signifiers of solidity (tissue, particles and pulses) and airiness (breath and atmosphere), ultimately overlaying or blending these seemingly distinct registers.
6. See Dames (2007) and Morgan (2017).
7. See Rudy (2009) and Hall (2017).
8. The best recent literary biography of Vernon Lee is Colby (2003).
9. A very helpful account of Lee's relation to these psychological traditions is given in Burdett (2011).
10. Lee (1881, 225).
11. Ibid., 226.
12. Ibid., 227.
13. Ibid., 229.
14. Ibid., 12–13.
15. Ibid., 10–11.
16. Lee (1933, 23). Music, Lee acknowledges, is the exemplary art form here, and the "clue to the study of all other branches of art," since its material "evanescence" establishes mostly clearly that art is definable as the "special group of responses which it is susceptible of awakening in the mind of its audience."
17. The relevant well-known passage from Pater's "Preface" to *Studies in the History of the Renaissance* reads: "in aesthetic criticism the first step towards seeing one's object as it really is, is to know one's own impression as it really is, to discriminate it, to realise it distinctly" (Pater 1873, viii). Pater's stress on knowing and defining one's impressions (suggesting an inner representational theatre) should, I suggest, be distinguished from Vernon Lee's emphasis on sensorimotor movements and reflex action (like respiration) which may occur either unconsciously or as conscious feeling, and this matters to her view of aesthetic experience as a mode of action rather than (I claim) representation.
18. The phrase is Pater's, from an essay on Coleridge originally published in 1866, in which he defines modern thought by its "relative spirit" and declares Coleridge, in contrast, to have been enslaved by the absolute. See Pater (1889, 65–67). For an exploration, and a defence, of relativism in nineteenth-century culture and ideas, see Herbert (2001).

19. Hannah (2013, 54).
20. Pater speaks of "that thick wall of personality through which no real voice has ever pierced on its way to us, or from us to that which we can only conjecture to be without [i.e. outside us]" (Pater 1873, 209).
21. Unless otherwise stated, I intend the term "cognition" to encompass more than rational behavior, knowing, reasoning, reflecting, problem-solving and so forth, and for it to be applied in the flexible fashion of many leading philosophers and cognitive theorists, particularly those interested in embodied cognition; for a helpful discussion of the "open-door policy" on what counts as cognition, see Wheeler (2005, 3–5).
22. For responses to the charge of solipsism levelled against Pater's aestheticism, see Levine (2000) and Morgan (2010), both of whom discuss Pater's interests in Victorian science and materialism. Vernon Lee's concept of aesthetic empathy, informed by the notion of feeling-into (*Einfühlung*) developed by the German philosopher Robert Vischer, is discussed in the following section of the chapter. My claim about active coupling, which draws on approaches to the mind labelled as "4E" theories of cognition (embodied, embedded, enactive and extended), is developed in the third section.
23. Morgan (2017, 153).
24. Wharton (1903, 513).
25. Huxley (1866, 285–286). See also Winter (1998, 327–328).
26. Huxley (1866, 285).
27. Carpenter first used unconscious cerebration in his *Principles of Human Physiology* (1854), though it tends to be associated with his popular book, *Principles of Mental Physiology* (1874). The idea was widely adopted. For a wide-ranging discussion of it under the rubric of "thinking without thinking," in Victorian intellectual life and in the novel, see Ryan (2012). Ryan, interestingly, does not mention Vernon Lee in this connection.
28. Dallas (1866, 243).
29. Ibid., 243.
30. Lewes (1859–1860, 2: 198).
31. Lewes (1859–1860, 1: 403–404).
32. Bain (1872, 15).
33. Dallas (1866, 245).
34. Ibid., 259.
35. Ibid., 242–243. Gertrud Mara (1749–1833) had been a court singer for Frederick the Great before making her London debut in 1784 and was widely praised for the brilliance of her vocal technique.
36. Ibid., 242.
37. Ibid., 243. Dallas quotes a lengthy corroborating passage from Ruskin's *The Two Paths* (1859) at the end of this part of *The Gay Science*.

38. Ruskin (1903–1912, 16: 419).
39. Ruskin (1903–1912, 16: 376–378).
40. Ruskin (1903–1912, 16: 383, 384).
41. If not quite gushing, Dallas makes no effort to disguise his high estimation of Ruskin's rhetorical style and "clear-seeing mind" in *Modern Painters* (1843–60) and his "magnificent" theory of the imagination (Dallas 1866, 192–193).
42. See Morgan (2017, 28–29).
43. Ruskin (1903–1912, 19: 360), my emphasis.
44. Lee (1913, 63). See also Keen (2007, 55–56).
45. Identification, Frow suggests, has been inflected by historical discourses of sympathy (and empathy), since the eighteenth century, whereas "affective investment may be positive or negative, and indeed encompasses a range of possible relations to characters, including dislike and indifference" (Frow 2014, 37–38).
46. Lee (1913, 69).
47. Ibid., 65–66.
48. As David M. Craig has argued, Ruskin's corrective for the pathetic fallacy—that is, for the failings of pathos manifested in bending objects to the perceiver's will—was reverence, and my own contention is that Vernon Lee's understanding of aesthetic empathy in 1913 retains an important sense of reverential self-abnegation, if in a different rhetorical register (see Craig 2006, 136).
49. Lee (1913, 68). See Lakoff and Johnson (1980).
50. Lee (1913, 139–140).
51. Lee and Anstruther-Thomson make this clear quite early on in their essay "Beauty and Ugliness," originally published in 1897 in the *Contemporary Review* (see Lee and Anstruther-Thomson 1912, 170–171). Here, they are making an implicit reference to Grant Allen, who had opened his *Physiological Aesthetics* (1877) by attacking Ruskin's failure in volume one of *Modern Painters* (1843) to say why certain visual forms bring pleasure. Lee and her collaborator, it should be noted, are choosing not to side not with Allen, who used evolutionary theory to explain this, but rather with Ruskin. They quote Ruskin's dictum that "beauty and ugliness are as positive in their nature as pleasure and pain," from *Modern Painters* III (Ruskin 1903–1912, 5: 45). On Lee and Allen, see also Burdett (2011).
52. Lee (1913, 109).
53. *The Beautiful* contains this moment of mild, if sincere, anti-bourgeois snobbery: "The very worst attitude towards art is that of the holiday-maker who comes into its presence with no ulterior interest or business, and nothing but the hope of an aesthetic emotion which is most often denied him" (Lee 1913, 138).
54. Lee and Anstruther-Thomson (1912, 154).

55. See Burdett (2011).
56. Lee and Anstruther-Thomson (1912, 163–164).
57. Ibid., 168–169.
58. How this occurs remains unclear, in virtue of its inaccessibility to introspection: "This realisation of distance is greatly reinforced by the adjustments taking place in the diaphragm. We do not pretend to explain what is really taking place in our body" (ibid., 213–214).
59. Ibid., 204.
60. Ibid., 224–225.
61. Ibid., 230–231, 280.
62. This example is discussed at length in Noë (2012).
63. Noë (2012, 80).
64. Krueger (2011, 9).
65. Hayles (2017, 62).
66. The opening section of the book, on "Aims and Methods," sets itself against Bertrand Russell and any other "Improbable Reader" who doubts such introspective methods (Lee 1933, 18–20).
67. Lee (1881, 11).
68. Dames (2007, 49).
69. Lee (1881, 106), my emphasis.
70. Ibid., 119 (emphasis added).
71. Noë (2015, 188).
72. Krueger (2011, 13).
73. This is not, I think, to beg the question by reducing musical sound to something in the head, a view that Noë in *Strange Tools* calls "subjective, interior, neurological," identifying it with neuroscientists like Daniel Levitin who insist, for example, that *pitch* refers to mental representation since sound waves do not themselves possess pitch (Noë 2015, 183).
74. Pater (1893, 245).
75. Ibid.
76. Lee and Anstruther-Thomson (1912, 80).

REFERENCES

Bain, Alexander. 1872. *Mental and Moral Science*, vol. 1, 3rd ed. London: Longmans, Green.

Burdett, Carolyn. 2011. "The Subjective Inside Us Can Turn into the Objective Outside": Vernon Lee's Psychological Aesthetics. *19: Interdisciplinary Studies in the Long Nineteenth Century.* http://doi.org/10.16995/ntn.610.

Colby, Vineta. 2003. *Vernon Lee: A Literary Biography.* Charlottesville: University of Virginia Press.

Craig, David M. 2006. *John Ruskin and the Ethics of Consumption.* Charlottesville and London: University of Virginia Press.

Dallas, E.S. 1852. *Poetics: An Essay on Poetry*. London: Smith, Elder.
Dallas, E.S. 1866. *The Gay Science*, vol. 1. London: Chapman and Hall.
Dames, Nicholas. 2007. *The Physiology of the Novel: Reading, Neural Science, and the Form of Victorian Fiction*. New York: Oxford University Press.
Frow, John. 2014. *Character and Person*. Oxford: Oxford University Press.
Hall, Jason. 2017. *Nineteenth-Century Verse and Technology: Machines of Meter*. Basingstoke: Palgrave Macmillan.
Hannah, Daniel. 2013. *Henry James, Impressionism and the Public*. London and New York: Routledge.
Hayles, Katherine N. 2017. *Unthought: The Power of the Cognitive Nonconscious*. Chicago: University of Chicago Press.
Herbert, Christopher. 2001. *Victorian Relativity: Radical Thought and Scientific Discovery*. Chicago: University of Chicago Press.
Huxley, Thomas Henry. 1866. *Lessons in Elementary Physiology*. London: Macmillan.
James, Henry. 1963. *Selected Literary Criticism*, ed. Morris Shapira. Harmondsworth: Penguin.
Keen, Suzanne. 2007. *Empathy and the Novel*. Oxford: Oxford University Press.
Krueger, Joel. 2011. Doing Things with Music. *Phenomenology and the Cognitive Sciences* 10: 1–22.
Lakoff, George, and Mark Johnson. 1980. *Metaphors We Live By*. Chicago: University of Chicago Press.
Lee, Vernon. 1881. *Belcaro, Being Essays on Sundry Aesthetical Questions*. London: W. Satchell and Co.
Lee, Vernon. 1913. *The Beautiful: An Introduction to Psychological Aesthetics*. Cambridge: Cambridge University Press.
Lee, Vernon. 1933. *Music and Its Lovers: An Empirical Study of Emotional and Imaginative Responses to Music*. New York: E. P. Dutton.
Lee, Vernon, and Clementina Anstruther-Thomson. 1912. *Beauty and Ugliness and Other Studies in Psychological Aesthetics*. London: John Lane and The Bodley Head.
Levine, George. 2000. Two Ways Not to Be a Solipsist: Art and Science, Pater and Pearson. *Victorian Studies* 43 (1): 7–41.
Lewes, George Henry. 1859–1860. *The Physiology of Common Life*, 2 vols. Edinburgh and London: William Blackwood and Sons.
Morgan, Benjamin. 2010. Aesthetic Freedom: Walter Pater and the Politics of Autonomy. *ELH* 77 (3): 731–756.
Morgan, Benjamin. 2017. *The Outward Mind: Materialist Aesthetics in Victorian Literature and Science*. Chicago: University of Chicago Press.
Noë, Alva. 2012. *Varieties of Presence*. Cambridge: Harvard University Press.
Noë, Alva. 2015. *Strange Tools: Art and Human Nature*. New York: Hill and Wang.

Pater, Walter. 1873. *Studies in the History of the Renaissance*. London: Macmillan.
Pater, Walter. 1889. Coleridge. In *Appreciations, with an Essay on Style*, 64–106. London: Macmillan.
Pater, Walter. 1893. *On Plato and Platonism: A Series of Lectures*. London: Macmillan.
Rudy, Jason. 2009. *Electric Meters: Victorian Physiological Poetics*. Athens, OH: Ohio University Press.
Ruskin, John. 1903–1912. *The Complete Works of John Ruskin*, ed. E.T. Cook and Alexander Wedderburn, 39 vols. London: George Allen.
Ryan, Vanessa. 2012. *Thinking Without Thinking in the Victorian Novel*. Baltimore: Johns Hopkins University Press.
Wharton, Edith. 1903. The Vice of Reading. *North American Review* 177: 513–521.
Wheeler, Michael. 2005. *Reconstructing the Cognitive World: The Next Step*. Cambridge: MIT Press.
Winter, Alison. 1998. *Mesmerized: Powers of Mind in Victorian Britain*. Chicago: University of Chicago Press.

Open Access This chapter is licensed under the terms of the Creative Commons Attribution 4.0 International License (http://creativecommons.org/licenses/by/4.0/), which permits use, sharing, adaptation, distribution and reproduction in any medium or format, as long as you give appropriate credit to the original author(s) and the source, provide a link to the Creative Commons license and indicate if changes were made.

The images or other third party material in this chapter are included in the chapter's Creative Commons license, unless indicated otherwise in a credit line to the material. If material is not included in the chapter's Creative Commons license and your intended use is not permitted by statutory regulation or exceeds the permitted use, you will need to obtain permission directly from the copyright holder.

CHAPTER 5

Ebb and Flow: Breath-Writing from Ancient Rhetoric to Jack Kerouac and Allen Ginsberg

Stefanie Heine

Abstract Following the path of Charles Olson, Jack Kerouac and Allen Ginsberg negotiate breath as a compositional principle for a new particularly American literature. Such a poetics of breathing turns out to be a revival of classical thought. For ancient rhetoricians, especially Aristotle, Cicero and Quintilian, the breath-pause is constitutive for structuring speech. Already in the ancient approaches, a dilemma emerges: breathing is supposed to cut speech into well-measured units while physical respiration tends to be irregular. Even though the Beat poets seem to elude this problem in their attempt to adapt composition to the writer's individual rhythms, breath, as they theorise it, is a point where bodily processes and cultural techniques intersect. The natural, organic body as Kerouac and Ginsberg celebrate it invokes a cultural memory, and thus, the idea of a purely embodied writing is upset.

Keywords Breath · Embodied poetics · Jack Kerouac · Allen Ginsberg · Ancient rhetoric

> Verse now, 1950, if it is to go ahead, if it is to be of *essential* use, must, I take it, catch up and put into itself certain laws and possibilities of the breath, of the breathing of the man who writes as well as of his listenings.[1]

The opening claim of Charles Olson's influential essay "Projective Verse," already touched upon in the introduction of this book, responds to a set of questions that would occupy two circles of avant-garde writers in the 1950s and 1960s, the Black Mountain poets and the Beat movement: How can a new literature that radically breaks with tradition be inaugurated? What basis can it have, if not tradition? "The laws and possibilities of the breath," a recourse to "natural" bodily processes, promises freer expression and an emancipation of American poetry from old, formal conventions. Liberating language from the shackles of fossilised, dusty rules of metre and rhyme will vivify and renew it, while transferring the author's breathing rhythm to that of the words written will produce an organic, embodied literature that reconciles art and life. In his discussion of breath, Olson refers to the "revolution of the ear,"[2] pointing to a revival of orality in American poetry starting from Walt Whitman and extending to Ezra Pound and William Carlos Williams. His claims that "breath allows *all* the speech-force of language back in" and "speech is … the secret of a poem's energy"[3] could be read as a call for spoken literature, for words carried by physical breath, which are more lively than those "which print bred."[4]

For a number of writers of both the Beat and Black Mountain context, "speech-force" was not only to be realised in oral performances, but should also affect the words in the composition process, in which breath would function as a measure that is "arriv[ed] at … organically."[5] Olson, like Allen Ginsberg,[6] establishes a simple compositional principle: break the line when you run out of breath:

> And the line comes (I swear it) from the breath, from the breathing of the man who writes, at the moment that he writes, … for only he, the man who writes, can declare, at every moment, the line its metric and its ending—where its breathing, shall come to, termination.[7]

Similarly, Jack Kerouac proposes that a dash shall indicate the moment between inhalation and exhalation, when breath is drawn, replacing the commas and colons that more commonly separate grammatical and semantic units.[8] In these approaches, "preconceived metrical pattern[s]" are counteracted with more irregular, variable and individual structures derived from "a source deeper than the mind … the breathing and the belly and the lungs."[9]

Ancient Origins of the Breath-Stop

What was advocated as a fresh principle for a new literature in the essays, writing manuals and oral comments of the Beat and Black Mountain writers was actually a tacit renascence of classical thought. In ancient rhetoric, the importance of breathing as a bodily prerequisite for oral delivery and as a structuring element of speech was stressed by Aristotle, Cicero and Quintilian. Breath had a pivotal role in the creation of prose rhythm, which the rhetoricians considered as more loosely measured than poetry. Prose should be structured in sequences, for example "periods," which Aristotle defines as "sentence[s] that [have] a beginning and an end in [themselves]."[10] In line with the compositional ideas of the Beat and Black Mountain writers, for the rhetoricians breathing marks the intervals between structural sequences. Aristotle mentions that a period should be delivered "in a breath … taken as a whole"[11] and Cicero asserts that "there should be in speeches closes [of periods] where we may take breath."[12]

The period in ancient rhetoric is a clearly defined unit: a segment that represents a thought with a beginning and an end. This idea is taken up by Ginsberg and Kerouac. Ginsberg claims that the "[b]reath-stop and the thought-division could be the same,"[13] and Kerouac observes that a jazz musician blows "a phrase on his saxophone till he runs out of breath, and when he does, his sentence, his statement's been made … . That's how I therefore separate my sentences, as breath separations of the mind."[14] With the assumption that a unit of breath coincides with a unit of thought or a completed statement, Kerouac and Ginsberg consciously or unconsciously follow the rhetoricians.[15] What Kerouac and Ginsberg designate as a poetics of the body meets an old matter of controversy around the sound execution of artistic composition and sometimes unpredictable physical needs. The question arising for the ancient rhetoricians, Kerouac and Ginsberg, is: How does the necessity of drawing a breath while speaking undercut claims to a synchronicity of breathing and thinking?[16]

The reflections of the rhetoricians indicate that a seamless coincidence of sense and breath units cannot be taken for granted.[17] In Quintilian's detailed account of how a speech should be delivered orally, it becomes obvious that an exact concurrence of breathing pause and the completion of a period are only an aspirational ideal.[18] The rhetoricians generally argue that the completion of a period should determine the moment when a breath is drawn, and not the other way round. Cicero stresses that only the "unskilful and ignorant speaker … measures out the periods of his speech, not with art, but with the power of his breath."[19] He argues that the breathing pause should be motivated by coherent segments of speech rather than the bodily need to inhale: "there should be in speeches closes [of periods] where we may take breath not when we are exhausted, … but by the rhythm of language and thoughts."[20] Quintilian notes that the orators can train their breath through physical exercise in order to make it more amenable to the need to mark a period: "we ought to exercise it [the breath, or breathing], that it may hold out as long as possible."[21]

In this respect, Kerouac's and Ginsberg's position is diametrically opposite: the physical need to draw a breath shall determine the interval between thoughts and constitute the structural unit. To repeat, Ginsberg claims that the measure of the breath-stop is "arriv[ed] at … organically" and rhythmical structures come from "a source deeper than the mind … the breathing and the belly and the lungs." Kerouac stresses that he separates his phrases when he "draw[s] a breath"[22] like the saxophonist does when "he runs out of breath."[23] However, their commitment to what Cicero designates as rude oratory does not resolve the tension between the physical necessity to inhale and the breathing pause as a structuring principle of speech already present in antiquity. The units of thoughts and statements addressed by Kerouac and Ginsberg undermine their claim of a compositional principle solely generated from the body. In the reference to the coincidence of breathing and structural units, the "nature" of their compositional theories as a *cultural* inheritance becomes obvious; the unaddressed yet distinctly audible resonances with ancient rhetoric alone unsettle the idea of an art that comes to be in a fully organic manner. In the context of their writings, breath does not only refer to the *body* "of the man who writes," but also back to a *rhetorike techne* in which they are engaged. What is proposed as a means to approach a reconciliation of art and life in fact turns out to be a discursive vitalism pointing to an older discourse and cultural technique in which a seamless coincidence of body and artistic composition has already been challenged.

Against the background of this incongruity, this chapter traces the contradictions of Ginsberg's and Kerouac's notions of a vital, bodily breath-writing. In the comments about their writing process, neither Ginsberg nor Kerouac give a clear definition of what the proposed segments, the "mind-breaks" or "thought-divisions" in Ginsberg's case, and the "phrases," "sentences" or "statements" in Kerouac's case actually consist in.[24] Whether the two writers actually did break up their lines or sentences when they had to inhale is impossible to verify in written documents. While one can check drafts and manuscripts for where line-breaks are made and where dashes or other pause markers are inserted, this textual geneticism does not demonstrate Kerouac's and Ginsberg's actual breathing patterns.[25] Moreover, their poetics of breath rests on collapsing a fundamental difference between oral and written composition. What the ancient rhetoricians have in mind is a scenario of oral composition: the orator composes his sentences as he speaks. In contrast, Ginsberg and Kerouac primarily composed in writing: by hand or with a typewriter. When the writer "pronounces" the words in his head while writing, a need to inhale does not necessarily coincide with the moment where a breathing pause would have occurred if the same sentence were spoken. In fact, we may place many more words in the span of one breath if we pronounce them in our head than if we pronounce them orally.[26] In contrast to oral composition, in writing, composition is not inevitably affected by the necessity to draw a breath: while writing, one can inhale without this effecting a pause in the sentence put on paper. When breath-measure is applied to written composition, its organic foundations disappear. Concerning Kerouac's and Ginsberg's texts, one observation is obvious: the pause markers almost always seamlessly coincide with grammatical units—so either the "laws … of the breath" were ignored in the actual writing process, or they do not structure speech differently to standard grammatical units. Moreover, if a healthy body also "unconsciously" follows the control of the mind to such a degree that breathing adjusts itself to anticipated syntactic breaks, the "laws of the breath" may actually (and unintentionally) be the "laws of the mind" rather than "a source deeper than the mind."[27]

The only documented cases where Ginsberg adopted an oral compositional technique are his so-called auto-poesy tapes. In a lecture, Ginsberg later explicates his recording compositions in terms of his theory of the mind- and breath-stop:

> most machines have a "stop" and a "start" button …, so if you're actually intending to do writing, one way is to use the automatic "control" button as the margin of your line … . That is, you're talking into the machine, you don't have anything to say, so you click it off. Then, when something

> emerges, when you notice something ... – click! Then, when you're transcribing on a page, ... which I've done a lot, from '65 to'70, with a Uher machine, you can use the "click" at the end of the tape line, the tape operation, as your breath stop. ... [I]t's the natural end of the line.[28]

An investigation of the tapes archived at Stanford University shows that what Ginsberg presents here is indeed a theory—a theory that does not match his compositional practice. Not only does he rarely use the stop and start buttons during composition, but the pauses in the recordings do not always coincide with the line-breaks in the printed poems. In most cases, it is unlikely that the pauses mark moments where Ginsberg ran out of breath; they rather indicate points where he ran out of thought: often, he only speaks two or three words, followed by very long intervals during which numerous breaths can be taken, often punctured by interjections like "ahem." Consequently, when Ginsberg designates the "natural" end of a line as "breath-stop" in retrospect, he uses the term as an *image* for the mind-break, or as a *name* for the line-break in the written text (note that in the lecture, he comes up with breath in the context of transcribing the spoken poem), which has little to do with his actual breathing during composition.

Following these observations, it has to be stressed that Kerouac's and Ginsberg's reflections of breathing and writing are poetological theories rather than descriptions of actual composition processes. While it is worth considering these in their own right, it is important to be aware of the ambivalent position bodily breath thereby comes to occupy: while it is celebrated as the natural source of a literary text's structure, its actual role in the writers' compositional practices seems to be marginal. Bearing this ambivalence in mind, I will elucidate the particularities of Kerouac's and Ginsberg's poetics of breathing, whose fixation on vitalism turns out to be grounded more in discourse than in physiology. The trajectories of their respective poetological endeavours become explicit when counterpointed against theories of rhetorical composition. Thus, I want to pair Ginsberg with Quintilian and Kerouac with Aristotle, focusing especially on the character and function of the caesura.

Ginsberg and Quintilian

Ginsberg claims that the so-called natural speech pauses, which he identifies with "breath-stops," "indicate mind-breaks."[29] The "[b]reath stop is where you stop the phrase to breathe again. Stop to *think* and breathe."³⁰ By claiming that "you're gonna stop and take a breath" when "you run out of thought and words,"³¹ he recalls Quintilian, who argues that the pause is the "point, where the mind takes a breath and recovers its energy."³² For Quintilian, the breathing pause is the moment "when the rush of words comes to a halt"³³ and the mind is relieved from its work. The pause should provide a rest so that the orators can assemble their mental forces anew before the next compositional effort. When claiming that the mind takes a breath, Quintilian deploys a metaphor invoking the intake of vital breath.³⁴ He addresses the "rush of the words" the pause interrupts and thus recalls a common association tied to the metaphor of "taking a breath" in the sense of relaxing: slowing down, i.e. the pace of one's breathing rhythm. To do nothing except breathe seems to suggest that one does almost nothing: "taking a breath" is "pausing." The image of the mind taking a breath during the pause implicates that the mind stops doing what it usually does, namely thinking. By claiming that the mind takes a breath in the moment of the breathing pause, Quintilian rhetorically establishes a temporal coincidence of metaphorical breath and its literal, or, precisely speaking non-linguistic, bodily referent.

In his remarks on the breathing pause and writing, Ginsberg also tries to reconcile metaphorical and literal dimensions of breathing. In the sentence "when you talk and then after a while you run out of thought and words, … then you're going to stop and take a breath and continue," Ginsberg synchronises the metaphor of "taking a breath"³⁵ with physical inhalation. Like Quintilian, he suggests that the breathing pause between uttered words (literally taking a breath) is a moment of rest and recovery (metaphorically taking a breath)—and that the mind needs to rest when the speaker runs "out of thought." Ginsberg also addresses the other implications of "taking a breath," discussed in Quintilian's use of the metaphor: inhaling vitalising air and doing almost nothing. He states that during the pause, the writer is "waiting for the next thought to articulate itself."³⁶ By noting "you're improvising and you're relying on the moment-to-moment inspiration,"³⁷ Ginsberg suggests that physical inspiration, inhaling, coincides with inspiration in the classical sense: the generation of creative ideas. The metaphorical breath of life as a vitalising force is thus transferred to the domain of artistic work in process. Drawing on his preoccupation with Buddhist thought and meditation practices, Ginsberg considers it relevant that ideas are generated where *nothing* is written or thought. The "blank spots," or "gaps in between the thoughts,"³⁸ Ginsberg addresses in this context overlap exactly with the point where he locates the breath-stop. Out of the "unborn awareness,"[39] a space of pure potentiality that opens in the moment when we do nothing but breathe, new thoughts are generated. The conflation of the physiological process of breathing, that is, the so-called natural pause or breath-stop and the mind-break, with the emergence of new ideas, that is, inspiration, becomes most noticeable in his "Notes on *Howl*": "Ideally each line of Howl is a single breath unit … —that's the Measure, one physical-mental inspiration of thought contained in the elastic of a breath."[40]

Even though Ginsberg encourages his readers to take both the metaphor of "taking a breath" and the notion of inspiration literally, his theory pushes physical respiration into the background. The claim that breath is a "source deeper than the mind" is made plausible in Ginsberg's comments on thought-generating "unborn awareness." However, reconciling breathing and inspiration in this way does not explain why the end of a thought should coincide with the need to draw a breath. The neat outline of "breath-stop=mind-break=inspiration" is an attempt to bring the body into agreement with compositional techniques, traditional ideas about how creative works are generated and theories of thought processes. Such a carefully constructed model—clearly a work of a well-read mind—stands in conflict with the claim that the work of the respiratory organs, which proceeds according to its own mechanisms, is supposed to generate the rhythmical structures of the poem in process. The fact that breathing rhythms are influenced by accidental external circumstances and the respective bodily condition of the breather—which, quite surprisingly for a position that supposedly foregrounds the body, is never addressed by Ginsberg—counteracts the idea that "mind-breaks" should necessarily be "*identical* with natural speech pauses."[41] On the one hand, it is precisely the irregularity of breathing that makes it interesting for Ginsberg's polemic towards a new poetry: he stresses that, in contrast to the "automatic and mechanic," symmetrical and "even" measure of traditional metrical forms, poetry as he envisages it, "speech as breath from the body," is more variably structured.[42] On the other hand, the irregularities of a human's breathing rhythm run counter to the smooth symmetry Ginsberg establishes in his compositional theory. Ginsberg considers the work of the mind as a process which is at the same time bodily and intellectual.[43] His negotiations of breath and mind-breaks thus challenge a simple binary between a rational, intellectual mind and an irrational, animalistic body. However, the cost of this by all means productive questioning of a dualism that keeps haunting the Western world is an eradication of difference: Ginsberg seals the gap between mind and body that especially articulates itself when the body speaks, or to be precise, breathes. He claims that mind-breaks are *the same* as non-metaphorical breath-stops, that is, the pauses between inhalation and exhalation in the physical respiration process.

Kerouac and Aristotle

Kerouac first and foremost links breathing to the free mind-flow and uncensored expression:

> PROCEDURE ... sketching language is undisturbed flow from the mind of personal secret idea-words, *blowing* (as per jazz musician) on subject of image.

> SCOPING Not "selectivity" of expression but following free deviation (association) of mind into limitless *blow-on-subject seas of thought*, swimming in sea of English with no discipline other than rhythms of rhetorical exhalation and expostulated statement ... —*Blow as deep as you want*— write as deeply, fish as far down as you want.[44]

> CENTER OF INTEREST ... *blow!*—*now!*—*your* way is your only way— "good"—or "bad"—always honest ("ludicrous"), spontaneous, "confessional" interesting, because not "crafted."[45]

The most obvious basis for the comparison of mind-flow and breath is a term Kerouac adopts from jazz music: "blowing." In jazz, "blowing" refers to improvisation.[46] In the case of the improvised saxophone-solo Kerouac addresses in his *Paris Review* interview, such an improvisation is literally blown. With respect to the breath-carried sounds produced by the saxophonist and, by analogy, by the speaker who improvises literary texts, Kerouac's image has a physiological basis. However, the suggested continuity of the flow of the mind and breathing is as rhetorically constructed as Ginsberg's equation of breath-stop and mind-break. This analogy is informed by the idea that physical breathing happens unconsciously and thus escapes from those grammatical and syntactical rules that restrict the mind's free expression—prohibitions the conscious mind cannot ignore. Further, the flow of exhaled air lends itself to a comparison with the *stream* of consciousness.

Kerouac extends the analogy between breath and a liberated mind to language: the free flow of the mind shall be mirrored in the free flow of language. Kerouac does not go so far as to propose a purely fluent, unsegmented speech or writing. His alternative is to replace the barriers of conventional punctuation mirroring grammatical units with a less restraining separator, namely breath.

> No periods separating sentence-structures already arbitrarily riddled by false colons and timid usually needless commas—but the vigorous space dash separating rhetorical breathing (as jazz musician drawing breath between outblown phrases)—[47]

While the ancient rhetoricians make a considerable effort to reconcile the breathing pause and grammatical units in their arguments, Kerouac is eager to separate the two. In ancient rhetoric, the image of flowing water, which Kerouac invokes in the "flow" and the "seas" of language, is used in order to depict what is spoken between the pauses: Quintilian mentions "the unbroken flow of the voice ... being carried along down the stream of oratory"[48] and Cicero compares ongoing speech with "the rolling stream of a river."[49] In both cases, the breathing pause is what brings that flow to a halt. Even though he takes the caesura into account, Kerouac's reservations against anything that disturbs the flow are apparent.

In the unpublished essay "History of the Theory of Breath as a Separator of Statements in Spontaneous Writing," Kerouac extends his comparison of breath-measure to jazz music: in a handwritten addition, the jazz musician is equated with both a runner and orator, and jazz is mentioned in the same breath with oratory and a hundred-yard dash. The imperative "write excitedly, swiftly"[50] became the foundation of the most prominent Beat and Kerouac-myth,[51] culminating in the repeatedly invoked scene of Kerouac taping together sheets of paper to a long scroll in order to avoid interruptions before manically typing down *On the Road* in three weeks.[52] In Kerouac's discussion of running, pausing and writing, we find a striking echo of Aristotle. Aristotle argues that, in contrast to a style segmented by periods, colons and commas, the loose or continuous style is "unpleasant, because it is endless, for all wish to have the end in sight."[53] He gives the following reason for the benefits of the pause: "runners, just when they have reached the goal, lose their breath and strength, whereas before, when the end is in sight, they show no signs of fatigue."[54] The advantage of the pause is that it prevents fatigue, the loss of breath, and that it impels the runner to go on. In his argument for pauses, Aristotle looks at them prospectively, as something that lies ahead. Such a prospective view opens a very attractive possibility for Kerouac: the break no longer blocks the flow, but generates an impetus to speed on. In a letter to his agent Sterling Lord, Kerouac stresses that the dashes indicating the breathing pause mark something impending: "Make this clear, that my prose is a series of rhythmic expostulations of speech visually separated for the convenience of the reader's eye by dashes, by vigorous definite dashes, which can be seen coming as you read."[55] Kerouac also highlights the importance of looking ahead during composition in "History of the Theory of Breath": analogous to the writer of spontaneous prose, the jazz musician has to keep track of breath when he moves from one chorus to the next in order to create a continuity between segments.

For Kerouac, the pause as such, the moment when according to Aristotle the runners "lose their breath and strength," represents the most delicate moment in his theory of writing. Whereas Ginsberg emphasises the meditative potentiality of the pause as a moment of calmness and rest, Kerouac is focused on the speed of the flowing words.[56] The idea of resting in the sense of slackening poses a threat to his obsession with mastery and an intact, potent masculine body mirrored in a muscular, virile prose.[57] The aspired athletic speed of writing should demonstrate vigour. Kerouac claims that he wants to write "[l]ike Proust, but on the run, a Running Proust."[58] "I decided to do just like he did—but fast. ... Fast. Marcel Proust had asthma and was lying around writing and eating in bed. Once in a while he'd get up feebly, put on a coat and go down a bar in Paris."[59] Just like Proust, Kerouac wants to write a monumental cycle of novels covering his entire life—but he neither wants to spend as much time as Proust did on the *Recherche*,[60] nor, most importantly, to fail in accomplishing the oeuvre. His comments show that in wishing to be a "running Proust," Kerouac also wanted to ensure that he didn't mimic Proust's frailty. What Kerouac aspires to is an athletic writing in contrast to an asthmatic one.[61] The breath Kerouac wishes to incorporate in his writing is one of a healthy, well-trained, potent body. It is significant that, in his emphasis on speed, Kerouac conceals the fact that a strained body may be out of breath, or that speaking on the run could be controlled by strained breath.[62] A breath that indicates signs of the body's slackening or weakens it, a writing structured by asthma attacks and apnoea would endanger Kerouac's poetological pursuits. In other words, Kerouac cannot envision breathlessness in his poetic theory. A physiological foundation of writing is only desirable if the body in question is intact and disciplined into athletic strength. Spontaneous writing as such is considered as a result of discipline, or, to follow Kerouac's own image, the runner's sprint provides an immediate demonstration of what rigorous training and hardening muscles give rise to.

> ... the critics have failed to realize that spontaneous writing of narrative prose is infinitely more difficult than careful slow painstaking writing with opportunities to revise—Because spontaneous writing is an ordeal requiring immediate discipline—They seem to think there's no discipline involved—They don't know how horrible it is to learn immediate and swift discipline and draw your breath in pain as you do so.[63]

Spontaneous prose is described as the empowering accomplishment of hard work. The aching breath recalling Shakespeare's *Hamlet*[64] results from the exertion of a well-trained body and stands in contrast to the painful asthmatic breath exhausting a body subject to illness. The reference to Proust's asthma and his debilitated physical condition shows Kerouac's longing for mastery over his body and writing alike: the healthy and strong body is a body under command.[65] The athlete's control over his muscles creates the illusion that he is liberated from the more random works of the body that may affect a person (i.e. illness). The imperatives of a "defective" body have no place in Kerouac's theory of writing.

Consequently, Kerouac invests the breathing pauses with implications forbidding any possibility that they may be a symptom of the fatigued body. In this respect, it is significant how he describes the graphical sign that should mark the breathing pause and its function:

> No periods separating sentence-structures already arbitrarily riddled by false colons and *timid* usually needless commas—but the *vigorous space dash* separating rhetorical breathing.[66]

> ... a sentence which after all is a rhetorical expostulation based on breathing and has to end, and I make it end with a *vigorous release sign*, i.e., the *dash*—[67]

By repeatedly describing the dash as "vigorous" (in contrast to the "timid" commas), Kerouac projects the strength of the runner into the pause, the moment when his body is in danger of collapsing and his muscles are bound to go limp. The aim of associating the pause with virility motivates the choice of the dash as the sign marking it on a semantic and graphical level: "dash" designates the punctuation mark Kerouac uses, but also the runner's sprint. Through the "dash," the pause develops a sense of speeding on. In Kerouac's handwritten manuscripts, the dashes also evoke an impression of speed graphically: often, the lines look as if they were dashed off energetically. Visually, the dash—in this case especially the printed one—establishes a proximity between words it separates: it links them by a vertical line almost touching their respective ends and beginnings, so that the eye is invited to follow this connection. Whereas a blank space between words encourages the eye to pause, the dash rather incites the eye to sprint between words. Moreover, in contrast to the bent commas and colons, the erect straight line of dash, which is also bigger in size, has a phallic quality. When his editor at the Grove Press, Don Allen, replaced dashes by full stops and added commas in the manuscript of *The Subterraneans*, Kerouac complained about this "horrible castration job." "He has broken down the organic strength of the manuscript and it is no longer THE SUBTERRANEANS by Jack K, but some feeble something by Don Allen."[68]

Such a castration anxiety also explains why Kerouac mingles images of breath and sex in the "Essentials":

> … write outwards swimming in sea of language to peripheral release and exhaustion—[69]
>
> … write excitedly, swiftly, with writing-or-typing-cramps, in accordance (as from center to periphery) with laws of orgasm … . Come from within, out—to relaxed and said.[70]

"[E]xhaustion," which in terms of respiration represents a threat—i.e. Proust's asthmatic feebleness and Aristotle's drained runner who has lost his "breath and strength"—is redirected to the domain of sexual climax: Kerouac links the "relaxed" moment of the pause to an explosive "release" of male (creative) potency. Kerouac repeatedly writes that the dashes "release" the sentence. Beside the sexual connotations evoked in the "Essentials," "release" also designates "liberation," the "action of freeing, or the fact of being freed." Moreover, in jazz music, "release" designates a "passage of music that serves as a *bridge* between repetitions of a main melody."[71] By choosing the word "release" in order to describe the function of the dash, Kerouac is able to connect all the qualities he wants to project into the breathing pause in order not to make it appear as slackening or escaping mastery: virility, liberation and a sense of continuity pointing forward to the point after the critical moment of the pause. The word also contains Kerouac's most eager wish: to make his writing available to the public, to release his written products, to get published and be honoured as America's healthy Proust. Kerouac's comments on his writing processes and methods, above all the "Essentials," were most important elements in his attempt to create a public image of himself as a writer. The potent, vigorously breathing body of the authoritative and controlling author Kerouac promotes is produced by his own words. Kerouac's literary texts are constructed in a way that evokes the impression of spontaneous, bodily, athletic writing executed by a vigorous author. The comments on the writing process and methods are designed to verify and confirm—and not least co-create—the effect produced in the literary texts.[72]

The texts by the ancient rhetoricians, Ginsberg and Kerouac, all imagine the writing or speaking body. In their discussions of the role of breath in writing, especially concerning the breathing pause, both Kerouac and Ginsberg follow in the footsteps of the rhetoricians. Whereas their poetological reflections start from the same premises, they ultimately diverge. Ginsberg's negotiation of the breathing pause amounts to a meditatively charged stasis, he emphasises the role of quiescent contemplation. Contrarily, Kerouac's poetics of breathing culminates in a promotion of flow, fast movement and virile athleticism.

Notes

1. Olson (1966, 15).
2. Ibid., 15.
3. Ibid., 20.
4. Ibid., 15. Even though Olson stresses orality in "Projective Verse," it is not his only concern, or even a primary one. As Raphael Allison notes in his book *Bodies on the Line: Performance and the Sixties Poetry Reading*, "competing with Olson's emphasis on the breath, graphic text itself was to him of equal value" (68). Prescient to the authors to be discussed in more detail in this article and their relation to orality, it has to be noted that Jack Kerouac did refer to spoken language and the tongue in his

comments on the new literature (e.g. in the unpublished essay "History of the Theory of Breath as a Separator of Statements in Spontaneous Writing") and did give public readings, but his overall focus has always been on writing and the written text. Allen Ginsberg's focus on the spoken word is much stronger: he repeatedly stresses its importance in his interviews (e.g. 2001, 81, 158, 272), and—as a grandfather of contemporary poetry slams—presenting his poetry orally to a live audience was a priority in his literary endeavours. The legendary reading of "Howl" at the Six Gallery is only one example.
5. Ginsberg (2001, 19).
6. "Ideally each line of Howl is a single breath unit. ... My breath is long—that's the measure, one physical-mental inspiration of thought contained in the elastic of a breath" (Ginsberg 1999, 416). "So you arrange the verse line on the page according to where you have your breath stop, and the number of words within one breath, whether it's long or short, as this long breath has just become" (Ginsberg 1997, 23).
7. Olson (1966, 19).
8. For example, Kerouac (1992, 57) and Kerouac (1999, 15).
9. Ginsberg (2001, 19).
10. Aristotle (1926, 389).
11. Ibid.
12. Cicero (1990, 506). I take this short summary of the role of breath in ancient rhetoric from my article "*animi velut respirant*. Rhythm and Breathing Pauses in Ancient Rhetoric, Virginia Woolf and Robert Musil."
13. Ginsberg (2001, 359).
14. Kerouac (1968).
15. Neither Ginsberg nor Kerouac explicitly refers to ancient rhetoric. It is also unclear whether they read the rhetoricians' discussions of breath or may have been familiar with their ideas through secondary sources.
16. Regarding the empirical perspective on this matter, a study conducted at Northeastern University by François Grosjean and Maryann Collins from 1979 approaching the question "What is the relationship between linguistic structure and breathing?" (100) concludes that breathing pauses "occur mainly at major constituent breaks" (110). "[T]he need to breathe (at least at slow and normal rates) is not in control of pausing but ... on the contrary, breathing adjusts itself to pause patterns" (109). Only when the participants of the study were asked to speak very fast, their breathing pauses did not coincide with syntactic breaks: at faster rates "the physiological need to breathe forces the speaker to stop in order to inhale," disregarding syntactic units (112). It has to be mentioned that the study is based on the speaking of healthy participants who were asked to read a text in which punctuation marks indicated where

the syntactic units are. Along with the fact that it is a quite old study, the results cannot be transferred seamlessly to the scenario of oral composition the rhetoricians and Beat and Black Mountain writers have in mind. However, it is revealing that breathing pauses and syntactic units seem to co-occur smoothly, but only as long as the body is under control, and that the physiological need to inhale tends to interrupt the syntax once the circumstances of the bodily condition for some reason changes.

17. Cicero attempts to conciliate the physical need to inhale and making a pause at the completion of a period by means of a quite constructed argument that beauty in artificial works is in agreement with natural utility (1875, 244).
18. Quintilian (1856, 352–353). Also in the passages on composition, there are uncertainties about the moment when a breath is required because a thought is completed at the moment when the orator should actually take a breath: "Who, for example can doubt that there is but one thought in the following passage and that it should be pronounced without a halt of breath? Still, the groups formed by the first two words, the next three, and then again by the next two and three, have each their own special rhythm and cause a slight check in our breathing" (Quintilian 1943, 545).
19. Cicero (1875, 243).
20. Cicero (1990, 506). The editor's comment to this passage shows that the rhetoricians' attempts to reconcile the completion of the period with the need to inhale leads to inconsistencies: "There is no real, though an apparent inconsistency: the periods must furnish opportunity for taking breath, but must not be determined solely by the need for this" (Cicero 1990, 506).
21. Quintilian (1856, 357). This overview of the breathing pause in ancient rhetoric is taken from my article *"animi velut respirant*. Rhythm and Breathing Pauses in Ancient Rhetoric, Virginia Woolf and Robert Musil."
22. Kerouac (1999, 15).
23. Kerouac (1968), not paginated.
24. Even though the examples Ginsberg uses as illustrations in numerous interviews and line-breaks or sentence segmentations in Ginsberg's and Kerouac's literary texts give some indication of these units, a precise explication is still lacking.
25. Investigating the breath-stops in their oral deliveries, in contrast, is possible in the cases where recordings were made. In Ginsberg's recordings of *Howl*, for example, one can observe that the moments when he inhales and pauses do not always coincide with the line breaks. Even though Ginsberg stresses that he imitates the compositional process in his readings (2001, 126), the readings as such do not constitute valid data for

an investigation of the composition process. The only thing one might infer from Ginsberg's *Howl* readings is that the moments when he has to inhale before the line ends show that his breath may not be as long as he claims in the *Notes for* Howl—even though he himself addresses this fact and attributes it to his exhaustion at the moment when he was reading (2001, 416).
26. This may explain Ginsberg's long lines in *Howl*, which he cannot pronounce in one breath orally (see 25).
27. See 16.
28. Ginsberg (1974).
29. Ginsberg (2001, 126).
30. Ibid., 108.
31. Ibid., 359.
32. Quintilian (1943, 543).
33. Ibid., 543.
34. The Latin use of "respire," the verb used by Quintilian, already included the figurative meaning of breathing as resting: "*to fetch one's breath again, to recover breath; to recover, revive, be relieved* or *refreshed* after any thing difficult (as labor, care, etc.)" (Lewis and Short 1879).
35. In the *Oxford English Dictionary*, "to take breath" is considered to be a figurative use of the "[p]ower of breathing, free or easy breathing": "to breathe freely, to recover free breathing, as by pausing after exertion" (*OED* online).
36. Ginsberg (2001, 126).
37. Ibid., 411.
38. Ibid., 365.
39. Ibid.
40. Ginsberg (1999, 416).
41. Ginsberg (2001, 126). In the Q&A session of lecture given in 1974, Ginsberg puts this claim into perspective and admits that his conceptions of mind units and breath units are not fully fleshed out. A student asked how Ginsberg uses his breath when he writes in a notebook: "do you read it out loud as you're writing it down?" In reply, Ginsberg mentions "It's an interesting thing whether it's breath or it's mind unit. I never figured that out" (Ginsberg 1974).
42. Ginsberg (2001, 107).
43. Ibid., 145.
44. Kerouac (1992, 57), my emphasis.
45. Ibid., 58, italics in the original.
46. Witmer (2003).
47. Kerouac (1992, 57).
48. Quintilian (1943, 541).

49. Cicero (1875, 247).
50. Kerouac (1992, 58).
51. Kerouac himself spent considerable efforts to create and maintain that myth, which for him goes hand in hand with having found his own style and "voice," most prominently expressed in the "Essentials." Significantly, the "Essentials" constitute an instruction to imitate, circulate and popularize the style Kerouac discovered for himself.
52. It has long been known that this is not an accurate description of how *On the Road* came to be and that Kerouac spent years taking notes and designing drafts for the novel (cf., for example Brinkley 2004, xxv).
53. Aristotle (1926, 387).
54. Ibid.
55. Kerouac (1999, 11).
56. Even though Ginsberg occasionally also refers to speed, for example by referring to the next line to be written or read as "next spurt" (2001, 125), this is never at the centre of his reflections—he rather seems to be echoing Kerouac's ideas of "athletic speech" (Ginsberg 2001, 114) in these instances.
57. Kerouac stresses these characteristics on a small undated scrap of paper containing a list of desirable prose attributes.
58. Kerouac (1995, 515).
59. Kerouac (2005, 192).
60. Kerouac (1995, 515).
61. See Benjamin (1968).
62. See 16.
63. Kerouac (1999, 325).
64. "Draw your breath in pain" is, of course, an implicit quote. Kerouac was well aware of Hamlet's last words: he quotes "Absent thee from felicity awhile," the line preceding "And in this harsh world draw thy breath in pain," in a letter to Ginsberg written in 1947 (1995, 122). Moreover, in a letter to Neal Cassady in 1950, Kerouac makes an explicit reference to *Hamlet*, precisely when he "discovers" the strenuousness of writing spontaneously in one's own voice: "My important recent discovery and revelation is that the voice is all. Can you tell me Shakespeare's voice per se?—Who speaks when Hamlet speaks? HAMLET, not Will Shakespeare …. You, man, must write exactly as everything rushes in your head, and AT ONCE. The pain of writing is just that" (1995, 233). It is important to note that these earliest thoughts on spontaneous prose, in which breath is not explicitly mentioned, are inspired by Hamlet's last sigh.
65. In Proust's *Recherche*, a notion of mastery is not absent. To the contrary, the narrator uses his illness as a means to exert control over the characters he interacts with. In particular, in *The Captive*, the house he cannot leave

due to his physical condition becomes a setting where Marcel can subject his lover Albertine to his supervision and bend her to his will as well as a stage for the dramas he directs. The space he is limited to because of his feeble physical condition is totally under Marcel's control, precisely because it is secluded from the contingencies of the outside world. In *Le Souffle coupé. Respirer et écrire*, François-Bernard Michel claims that asthma implies a closure of what is supposed to be open: the asthmatic closes his bronchia and thus conserves his air, he refuses to exhale (194). The intentionality insinuated in Michel's formulation is problematic, but it gets to the heart of Marcel's attempt of creating an enclosed space sealed from exposure to the outside. Thus, Proust's asthma represents a flip side to Kerouac's poetics of breathing. Not only are the two models of literary breathers similarly subject to mystification: the aesthetic idealisation of the fin de siècle decadent in Proust's case, the phallocentric, virile daredevil who lives fast and dies young in Kerouac's case. In contrast to the asthmatic, Kerouac's athletic writing embraces exhalation: "blowing" is the central respiratory movement for Kerouac, and it has to be noted that in contrast, he is deeply suspicious of inhalation, of everything that enters the body from without and is not his own. Through his focus on exhalation, Kerouac stages an extension of the self to the outside world and is equally paranoid of a possible interference of the outside with the self as Proust is. The analogy of his writing and sprinting supports this: as an anaerobic exercise, the sprint relies on energy resources stored in the body—it allows a momentary fantasy of not being dependent on an oxygen supply from without.

66. Kerouac (1992, 57), my emphasis.
67. Kerouac (1995, 324), my emphasis.
68. Kerouac (1995, 11).
69. Kerouac (1992, 58).
70. Ibid.
71. *OED* online, my emphasis.
72. For a more detailed analysis of how the "Essentials of Spontaneous Prose" themselves represent a deliberate attempt to create an effect of spontaneity that first had to be carefully prepared, see my article "First Thought, Best Thought. Improvisation bei Jack Kerouac und Allen Ginsberg." A look at Kerouac's manuscripts and drafts shows that the methods and techniques he proposes in his writing manuals and comments have never been consequently applied in his actual writing processes. I investigated a large bulk of materials at the Berg Collection of English and American Literature, among them drafts for *The Subterraneans*, *On the Road* and *Visions of Gerard*. A detailed discussion of these findings, however, exceeds the scope of this paper. Generally, it is worth noting that Kerouac

made extensive use of "timid commas" and hardly used the dashes in a consequential manner (to replace commas, colons or full stops); most of the times, one can find a mixture of dashes, commas and full stops. I want to give only one example that demonstrates how Kerouac retrospectively—and against his imperative "*no revisions*" (1992, 57)—aligned his texts to his own writing instructions: in order to highlight that he replaces full stops by dashes, he consequently changes lowercased words succeeding a dash into capitalized ones in the setting copy of *Visions of Gerard*.

REFERENCES

Allison, Raphael. 2014. *Bodies on the Line: Performance and the Sixties Poetry Reading*. Iowa, IA: University of Iowa Press.
Aristotle. 1926. *The "Art" of Rhetoric*, ed. and trans. John Henry Freese. London: William Heinemann.
Benjamin, Walter. 1968. The Image of Proust. In *Illuminations*, trans. Harry Zohn, intro. Hannah Arendt, 201–215. New York: Schocken Books.
"breath." OED Online. Oxford: Oxford University Press. www.oed.com. Accessed 13 Mar 2018.
Brinkley, Douglas (ed.). 2004. *Windblown World: The Journals of Jack Kerouac 1947–1954*. New York: Viking Penguin.
Cicero. 1875. *Oratory and Orators*, ed. and trans. J.S. Watson. New York: Harper & Brothers.
Cicero. 1990. *de Oratore libri tres*, ed. August S. Wilkins. Hildesheim: Georg Olms Verlag.
Ginsberg, Allen. 1974. *Spiritual Poetics II*. Lecture at the Naropa University. https://archive.org/details/Allen_Ginsberg_class_Spiritual_Poetics_part_2_July_1974_74P002. Accessed 12 Mar 2018.
Ginsberg, Allen. 1997. Allen Ginsberg: An Interview by Gary Pacernick. *The American Poetry Review* 26 (4): 23–27.
Ginsberg, Allen. 1999. Notes for *Howl* and Other Poems. In *The New American Poetry 1945–1960*, ed. Donald M. Allen, 414–420. Berkeley: University of California Press.
Ginsberg, Allen. 2001. *Spontaneous Mind: Selected Interviews 1958–1996*, ed. David Carter. New York: HarperCollins.
Grosjean, François, and Maryann Collins. 1979. Breathing, Pausing and Reading. *Phonetica* 36: 98–114.
Heine, Stefanie. 2014. First Thought, Best Thought. Improvisation bei Jack Kerouac und Allen Ginsberg. In *Improvisation und Invention. Momente, Modelle, Medien*, ed. Sandro Zanetti, 245–259. Zürich: Diaphanes.

Heine, Stefanie. 2017. *animi velut respirant*. Rhythm and Breathing Pauses in Ancient Rhetoric, Virginia Woolf and Robert Musil. *Comparative Literature* 69 (4): 355–369.

Kerouac, Jack. 1968. The Art of Fiction No. 41. *The Paris Review*. www.theparisreview.org/interviews/4260/the-art-of-fiction-no-41-jack-kerouac. Accessed 12 Mar 2018.

Kerouac, Jack. 1992. Essentials of Spontaneous Prose. In *The Portable Beat Reader*, ed. Ann Charters, 57–58. New York: Viking.

Kerouac, Jack. 1995. *Selected Letters, 1940–1956*, ed. Ann Charters. New York: Viking Penguin.

Kerouac, Jack. 1999. *Selected Letters, 1957–1969*, ed. Ann Charters. New York: Viking Penguin.

Kerouac, Jack. 2005. Dialogues in Great Books. In *Empty Phantoms. Interviews and Encounters with Jack Kerouac*, ed. Paul Maher, 184–202. New York: Thunder's Mouth Press.

Michel, François-Bernard. 1984. *Le Souffle coupé: Respirer et écrire*. Paris: Gallimard.

Olson, Charles. 1966. Projective Verse. In *Selected Writings*, ed. Robert Creeley, 15–26. New York: New Directions.

Quintilian. 1856. *Quintilian's Institutes of Oratory: Or, Education of an Orator in Twelve Books*, vol. II, trans. John Selby Watson. London: Bohn's Classical Library.

Quintilian. 1943. *Institutio Oratia*, trans. H.E. Butler. Cambridge: Harvard University Press.

"release." *OED* Online. Oxford: Oxford University Press. www.oed.com. Accessed 13 Mar 2018.

"respiro." *A Latin Dictionary*. 1879. Ed. Charlton T. Lewis and Charles Short. Oxford: Clarendon Press. Online Version. www.perseus.tufts.edu/hopper/text?doc=Perseus%3Atext%3A1999.04.0059%3Aentry%3Drespiro. Accessed 13 Mar 2018.

Witmer, Robert. 2003. Blow. In *The New Grove Dictionary of Jazz*, ed. Barry Kernfeld. *Grove Music Online, Oxford Music Online*: Oxford University Press. http://www.oxfordmusiconline.com. Accessed 13 Mar 2018.

Open Access This chapter is licensed under the terms of the Creative Commons Attribution 4.0 International License (http://creativecommons.org/licenses/by/4.0/), which permits use, sharing, adaptation, distribution and reproduction in any medium or format, as long as you give appropriate credit to the original author(s) and the source, provide a link to the Creative Commons license and indicate if changes were made.

The images or other third party material in this chapter are included in the chapter's Creative Commons license, unless indicated otherwise in a credit line to the material. If material is not included in the chapter's Creative Commons license and your intended use is not permitted by statutory regulation or exceeds the permitted use, you will need to obtain permission directly from the copyright holder.

CHAPTER 6

Combat Breathing in Salman Rushdie's *The Moor's Last Sigh*

Arthur Rose

Abstract This chapter considers how thinking about the postcolony often invokes a language of breathlessness. Moments of severe breathlessness in postcolonial literature and criticism give way to observations of more systemic distortions in breathing patterns. By tracing the breathing metaphors in Salman Rushdie's *The Moor's Last Sigh*, the chapter offers a literary rapprochement to these different understandings of postcolonial breathlessness, particularly in the work of Frantz Fanon. It demonstrates the importance of the breath metaphor for postcolonial literature. Reciprocally, such literature shows how the cultural baggage of these breath metaphors leads to forms of catachresis and markedness. The language of breath and breathlessness often conflates their overlapping meanings in health, hygiene and literature. This chapter shows how Rushdie's work helps to signal these overlapping significances.

Keywords Salman Rushdie · Breath · *The Moor's Last Sigh* · Frantz Fanon · *A Guide to Health* · Postcolonial literature

In the wake of the Black Lives Matter movement, any consideration of the literary value of breath must also address how its politics projects itself into the postcolony, thought broadly as a condition rather than a geographical locale.[1] "I can't breathe," repeated Garner as he was pinned to the ground in an illegal chokehold by a New York police officer. He was killed for what Tony Medina has called, "being black and breathing."[2] Ashon Crawley opens *Blackpentecostal Breath* by quoting Garner, calling the phrase one of the most striking expressions of the devaluation of black lives in the USA today.[3] But Crawley also finds in Garner's words an implicit challenge to think otherwise: "a desire for otherwise air than what is and has been given, the enunciation, the breathing out the strange utterance of otherwise possibility."[4] Under the aegis of "expressing experiences of hostile environments and efforts to make life within them more liveable," Jean-Thomas Tremblay argues in his review of Crawley's book, "breath" articulates the somatic effects of subordination but it also has an "impulse to create and sustain human relationships."[5] With this heightened attentiveness to breath in Black Life, it is perhaps unsurprising that more attention was paid to Frantz Fanon's descriptions of postcolonial breathlessness. In *Black Skins, White Masks*, Fanon had taken the cause of revolt in Indochina as being "because quite simply it was, in more than one way, becoming impossible for them [the colonised] to breathe."[6] By late 2014, Tremblay argues, "Fanon's claim was resurrected on social media, as an extended version of 'I can't breathe.'" Moreover, as Tremblay notes, "the subject of the claim had been adapted to a more general 'we': 'When we revolt it's not for a particular culture. We revolt simply because, for many reasons, we can no longer breathe.'"[7]

By revising Fanon's work, from "them" to "we," activists could testify to their own oppression, while also commenting critically and reflexively upon the conditions behind it. In so doing, they relied on a compelling politicised image: the person who can no longer breathe. Given the work this image is meant to do, and the sensitivity of this work, any purely aesthetic engagement with it poses something of an ethical dilemma. An aesthetic discussion of Black Lives Matter and Garner's death risks dissimulating the political importance of the former and the real anguish of the latter. So as to recall this context without appropriating it, I focus on another case of postcolonial breathlessness, where the sufferer himself has already mediated his breathlessness through literature: Salman Rushdie and his 1995 novel, *The Moor's Last Sigh*.

For, if a number of Rushdie's novels mark the unusual properties of breath in providing an interface between the physiological, the metaphoric and the linguistic, breath's permutations are perhaps most emphasised in *The Moor's Last Sigh*, a multigenerational saga about a family of spice merchants, as narrated by their last scion, Moraes Zogoiby.[8]

6 COMBAT BREATHING IN SALMAN RUSHDIE'S *THE MOOR'S LAST SIGH*

Breath is marked throughout Rushdie's *Sigh* from the playful opening sequences—"when you're running out of steam, when the puff that blows you onward is almost gone, it's time to make confession" (*MLS* 4)—to the final, implacable pilgrimage, made "in spite of these lungs that no longer do my bidding" (*MLS* 433). Many of the narrator's meditations refer explicitly to breath, a reminder to read the novel thematically and formally as Moraes's "last sigh." Given the emphasis it places on breath, the novel invites formal aesthetic responses to its meditations on the respiratory. But it also has a clear biographical connection. As Rushdie himself would recall in his memoir *Joseph Anton*, *The Moor's Last Sigh* was written during the fatwa, proclaimed by Ayatollah Khomeini in 1989. Like *The Moor's Last Sigh*, Rushdie is plagued by late-onset asthma, which comes to be associated with the loss of freedom he experienced under witness protection in *Joseph Anton*. When he told his security protection that he wanted to leave the house to accept the Mythopoeic Fantasy Award for *Haroun and the Sea of Stories* in 1992,

> he inhaled deeply. (His reward for giving up smoking was the arrival of late-onset asthma, so he was sometimes short of breath.) 'You see,' he said, 'I was under the impression that I am a free citizen of a free country, and it's not really for you to *allow* or not *allow* me to do anything.' … 'In this free country,' he said, 'I am not a free man.'[9]

Asthma brings together, in this passage, breath(lessness) and (a lack of) freedom. In *The Moor's Last Sigh*, a similar incident is given a more transhistorical purpose. Consider the moment when Moraes's father, Abraham, first hears the story of Boabdil the Unlucky ("Zogoiby"), the last Moorish king of Granada. Boabdil, as he exits the Alhambra, gives forth a sigh that marks the end of his kingdom and gives its name to Rushdie's novel. As he hears the story, Abraham feels "all the mournful weight of Boabdil's coming-to-an-end":

> Breath left his body with a whine, and the next breath was a gasp. The onset of asthma (more asthma! It's a wonder I can breathe at all!) was like an omen, a joining of lives across the centuries, or so Abraham fancied as he grew into his manhood and the illness gained in strength. (*MLS* 80)

Abraham takes the onset of his asthma to be "an omen," connecting his life to Boabdil's, across time. This is consolidated as Abraham grows, and his illness becomes more debilitating. Abraham can make this connection because Boabdil's sigh parallels his own experiences of asthma as a "whine" and a "gasp." Somatic modes of awareness, according to Thomas J. Csordas, are the "culturally elaborated ways of attending to and with one's body in surroundings that include the embodied presence of others."[10] Rushdie attends to the somatic effects of Abraham's breathlessness, but he also shows how Abraham attends *with* his breathlessness. "Attending to a bodily sensation," Csordas argues, "becomes a mode of attending to the intersubjective milieu that give rise to that sensation. Thus, one is paying attention with one's body."[11]

This is not a new way of thinking about literature and embodiment.[12] But it does permit us to think of breath in the novel as playing with multiple modalities of awareness. Abraham's asthma attack serves to navigate the system at work. The attack begins with an exhalation ("a whine"), followed by an inhalation ("a gasp"). This is the immediate moment of postcolonial breathlessness, brought on as a result of a sympathetic response to the displaced Boabdil. Abraham's is a physiological, not a cultural, connection across history: "[he] felt all the mournful weight of Boabdil's coming-to-an-end, felt it as his own" (*MLS* 80). This connection is immediate and particular: it simply becomes impossible for him to breathe. The extended effect of this sympathy is more damaging than productive, for both Boabdil and the Da Gama-Zogoiby clan.

Breath conjoins Abraham and Boabdil in a manner that follows the operations of Homi Bhabha's much-contested term, hybridity: "the interstitial passage between fixed identifications ... to entertain difference without an assumed or imposed hierarchy."[13] Hybridity offers opportunities to subvert that which might otherwise be simply mimicked, in order to form new epistemic modes of connection. Breath, then, might be an enabling condition for hybridity, since it acts as a conduit between the asthma of Boabdil and Abraham. But, as Atef Laoyene has demonstrated, Rushdie's "post-exotic" style demolishes postcolonial hybridity:

> Rushdie's postmodern superimposition of Andalusian history and India's national narrative in *The Moor's Last Sigh* is less a nostalgia for an exotic and lost Golden Age, as many Rushdie critics have suggested, than an attempt to map out the limits of postcolonial hybridity as an empowering subject position.[14]

The limits, for Laoyene, are expressed in Rushdie's attitude to Aurora's artwork: "its variations on the Andalusian theme do not foreground realistically enough the plight of India's masses."[15] "The Andalusian theme" might refer as much to Boabdil's influence on Abraham's asthma as on Aurora's art. Boabdil was forced to abdicate to Isabella of Spain, thus bringing an end to Moorish Spain and the *convivencia* (or "living together") between Christians, Jews and Muslims. The *convivencia* acts as a loose paradigm for subsequent celebrations of multiculturalism and hybridity. But, Laoyene argues, Rushdie's inclusion of "the Moor" does not aim to endorse these celebrations. It critiques them. Abraham's identification with Boabdil gives way to palimpsestic reproductions of Boabdil (by the artists, Vasco Miranda and Aurora), that eventually turns the Moor into a "phantasmagoric hollow man."[16] In keeping with this hollowness, the elevation of Abraham's moment of physiological crisis to the metaphysical matter of destiny leads to subsequent deformations suffered by the family. His postcolonial breathlessness is a physiological response that he elevates to a transcultural, transhistorical network of shared suffering. Abraham will use this physical fragility as the basis of his criminal empire, as "a mughal of human frailty" (*MLS* 182). Although Abraham's forays into the sex and drug trades have little to do with breath, the implication is that he recognises the ways of capitalising on human weakness through his own, physiological vulnerability. The reality of physiological crises, confirmed and consolidated through the somaticising body, is that they put into play a series of attitudes and behaviours with long-term social consequences.

A conventional biographical reading of Rushdie authorises this sense that breathlessness, rather than its consequences, forms the "real" substrate of the novel. But it is also a fancy. Abraham's whine-gasp is taken to be *like* Boabdil's last sigh. The solidarity of Abraham's momentary breathlessness acts as the "deferential complaisant surface," the "overneath," to his actual life as a criminal mastermind, ruling "a Mogambo-ish underworld" (*MLS* 180). Rushdie implies something like Fanon's connection between breathlessness and an absence of freedom when describing Abraham's asthma. But, if we attend simply to the somatic immediacy of moments like these, we risk ignoring the ways in which these moments highlight other, systemic problems with the postcolonial state.

The task then that faces us in discussing the image of breathlessness in postcolonial literature and thought is not, then, simply the immediate appearance of exacerbated breathlessness and its resolution. We must also consider how systems of breathlessness come to operate in more covert, insidious ways. In contrasting immediate breathlessness with its more systemic conditions, our reading of Rushdie is, again, anticipated by Fanon. When considering the role Algerian women played in the Algerian War of Independence, Fanon makes a brief aside that links the phenomenological effects of occupation to respiratory distress: "there is not occupation, on the one hand, and independence of persons on the other. It is the country as a whole, its history, its daily pulsation that are contested, disfigured ... under these conditions, the individual's breathing is an observed, an occupied breathing. It is a combat breathing."[17] If, in early Fanon, a postcolonial breathlessness was a refusal brought about the immediate inability to breathe, by late Fanon, colonial occupation is far more subtle in its imposition of distorted breathing patterns.[18] When daily life itself suffers from a disfigured pulsation, no simple liberation narrative can suffice. Fanon's variated breathing, a *poesis* under political pressure, implies a complex problem: the need to reconfigure the conditions of breathing, as much as any more overt resistance.

We can illustrate Rushdie's concern with a systemic distortion of breath by recalling, in our reading of the novel, Mahatma Gandhi's *Guide to Health* (1921/1946), where breath becomes the basis for developing Gandhi's ideological concerns with purity, pollution and contamination.[19] *The Moor's Last Sigh*, like *Midnight's Children* before it, is critical of Gandhi's "sentimental claptrap of spinning your own cotton and travelling third-class on the train" (*MLS* 54). Rushdie's response satirises the nativist elements of Gandhi's programme, which sought a return to pre-colonial modes of production. Following Joseph Alter's *Gandhi's Body*, we can consider both the spinning and the travelling as elements in a broader project of biopolitical control: "Gandhi's search for Truth was manifest in his biomoral politics and his experimentation ... must be understood as integral to his project of *satyagraha* as a whole."[20] Similarly, Srirupa Prasad shows how Gandhi's health protocols, particularly those given in *Guide to Health*, are important in understanding not simply his nationalist politics but his sustained attempt to contain, curtail or restrict his affective affinities: "If *swaraj* or self-rule entailed manipulation and mastery over the body and its physiological processes, such dominance was in essence command over the fluctuations of emotions as well."[21] Control the body and you control the affective self. Rushdie's satire seems well situated to follow this extension of Gandhi's social activism into discourses of biopolitical control. After all, Rushdie's characters are notoriously incapable of controlling themselves, precisely because their bodies let them down: think, for instance, of Aurora's rages, Flora's madness or Moraes's uncontrolled ageing (he ages twice as fast as the "norm"). Again, these afflictions come from their lack of control over their bodies, a lack of control that manifests as much in the formal profusions of Rushdie's relentlessly associative prose as in the characters it represents. After remarking that it is easier to breathe in than out, Moraes goes on to liken this to passive resistance: "As it is easier to absorb what life offers than to give out the results of such absorption. As it is easier to take a blow than to hit back" (*MLS* 53). The latter has a family resemblance to a phrase, attributed to Gandhi, in Mahadev Desai's 1931 account of the First Round Table Conference held to discuss India's constitution in 1930. Speaking to a group of children from London's East End, Gandhi "explains how it is better by far not to hit back than to return a blow for a blow."[22] *Satyagraha*, or "the Force which is born of truth," came to replace "passive resistance" in Gandhi's philosophy, because the former implied strength and an adherence to truth where the latter might be confused with weakness and makes no mention of truth. But, when Moraes, the narrator, talks about passivity, it is not in conjunction with strength or truth; he advocates passivity because it is "easier." In these terms, Rushdie reverses Gandhi's protocols for the healthy body as the stepping stone to the healthy nation: often the unhealthy body is precisely what indicates the ill health of the state.

Rushdie had already challenged Gandhi's correlation between the health of the body and of the state in *Midnight's Children*, where the Indian State is "twinned" to Saleem Sinai more in sickness than in health. But it is Saleem's constantly dripping nose that is particularly at odds with the protocols of *Guide to Health*: "nasal congestion obliged me to breathe through my mouth, giving me the air of a gasping goldfish; perennial blockages doomed me to a childhood without perfumes."[23] For Gandhi, "that man alone is perfectly healthy … whose nose is free from dirty matter."[24] This is not his sole marker of health, but it is sufficiently important that Gandhi will return to it numerous times over the course of the pamphlet, stressing both the need to keep the nose clean and "to breathe through the nose."[25] "The air which is inhaled through the nostrils is sifted before it reaches the lungs, and is also warmed in the process."[26] In fact, breathing through the nose is so important that people who find themselves breathing through the mouth should "sleep with a bandage around the mouth."[27] If it warms the breath, breathing through the nose also acts as a filter, "a sieve," for impurities in the air. In this, breath control fits into the wider biopolitical concern with purification and pollution in the *Guide*.[28]

Mary Douglas, in her seminal *Purity and Danger*, begins her analysis of pollution by defining dirt as "matter out of place."[29] Pollution, according to Douglas, is determined not by a substance's quiddity, but by its position. Pollution pollutes when it transgresses into forbidden places; it violates laws formulated for moral reasons, rather than for principles of hygiene. Douglas's thinking demonstrates just how morally based Gandhi's hygiene practices are.[30] Protecting the body from dirt requires a clear moral stance on what constitutes dirt. And while Gandhi's examples are scarcely questionable (he cites London's smog, for instance), they do draw on "biomoral" politics. The instance of London smog appears fairly innocuous, but the specific place, "London," has a significant political charge, given Gandhi's work to secure Indian Independence from Britain. *A Guide to Health*, first written in Gujarat for *Indian Opinion* in 1913, ostensibly gains a political element when it is historicised, that is, put into relation with time. Will Viney introduces his study of waste by expanding Douglas's remit to include time: "this insistence on spaces of waste can confuse and obscure the crucial influence that time has in our experience of and dealing with waste things. Waste is also (and in both senses of the phrase) matter out of time."[31] If both Douglas and Viney are ultimately more concerned with waste things, their arguments impact on how we assess Gandhi's ideological preoccupation with purity. For, while we should acknowledge the empirical importance of the hygienic practices he is proposing, these practices do rely on an epistemic practice where each thing is kept to its proper place and time. The nose has just such a responsibility for Gandhi: it protects the body from outside pollutants. For Rushdie, the nose abdicates this responsibility, since it has an affective relation with these supposed contaminants that registers both in space and in time.

In *The Moor's Last Sigh*, the nose is marked as a site of affective contamination. These contaminations may register in linguistic, economic, erotic and physiological ways, but they have corresponding affective consequences. Camoens, Moraes's grandfather, pronounces his name "Camonsh-through-the-nose" (*MLS* 9), marking the family's commitment to their Portuguese ("alien") roots. When Moraes's parents, Abraham and Aurora, first make love, they do so on some pepper sacks, imbuing their skin and sweat with the smell of pepper: "what had been breathed in from the air during that transcendent fuck" (*MLS* 90). Contaminants through the nose destabilise the moral callings of other characters: notably Flora, Abraham's mother, and Oliver D'Aeth, the comic, photophobic Anglican priest, are driven mad by the smell of pepper on the lovers. Ultimately, when Aoi Ue tells the story of defeated love, it is not the substantive matter of betrayal that she cites as the reason she leaves her husband, it is those "small habits" that makes her leave: "the relish with which he picked his nose" (*MLS* 425). Finally, the physiological effect of a blocked nose correlates to an open mouth. When Uma, Moraes's lover, kills herself, the Police Inspector forces Moraes to take the remaining suicide pill by grabbing his nose: "Airlessness demanded my full attention …. I yielded to the inevitable" (*MLS* 292). Here, Moraes yields to the inevitable urge to open his mouth and breathe. A similar correlation between closed nose and open mouth occurs at the property of Hindu Nationalist, Raman Fielding, where the guard, Sneezo, is "permanently bung-nosed and – perhaps in compensation – less tight-lipped" (*MLS* 366). Nasal blockages effect a loss of control over the mouth, both physiologically and psychologically. In each situation, the nose is not, or has ceased to be, an adequate sieve. It either fails to keep the body pure from contaminants in the air or manages to do so only by blocking itself from outside influences. In our discussion of somatic modes of attention, it became clear that, instead of turning bodily sensation into the symptom of some other condition, Csordas suggests a mode of attention that uses the body to pay attention to the world. By paying attention to phenomena like Camoens's name, Abraham and Aurora's shared odour, or Sneezo's bunged up nose, we are not simply reading symptoms of the deformations of colonialism; we are reading its effects as they are imprinted on vulnerable bodies.

Rushdie's concern with the nose reminds us that images of postcolonial breathlessness require us to attend equally to descriptions of immediate breathlessness and to the respiratory systems which underpin them. In order to exercise a postcolonial literary analysis of this work that is at least as attentive to form as it is to sociopolitical conditions, it is necessary subject Fanon's phrase, "combat breathing," to a more critical appraisal. Considered as a contested, disfigured daily pulsation, "combat breathing" might be recast as a form of chronic stress, whereby the protracted exposure to "a real or perceived threat to homeostasis or well-being … can cause pronounced changes in psychology and behaviour that have long-term deleterious implications for survival and well-being."[32] "Medicalising" the term risks evacuating from it the specific form it takes in Fanon's essay. In context, it appears in a passage which relates to Fanon's broader psycho-phenomenological project: "it is not the soil that is occupied …. French colonialism has settled itself in the very centre of the Algerian individual and has undertaken a sustained work of cleanup, of expulsion of self, of rationally pursued mutilation."[33] Fanon's epiphora suggests that the breathing of the occupied becomes a mangle that includes the immediate experience of the colonised subject, the long-term conditions of the colonial environment and the contestation of their "daily pulsation." Fanon's combat breathing is not, then, a protocol of military training or a medical diagnosis; it is the marker of a colonial distortion that includes subjects, environments and activities.

In this exposition, "combat breathing" might simply describe parallels between the breathing complaints of Moraes and his family, and their extended experience of those colonial, and postcolonial, distortions that constitute threats to their homeostasis. Albert Memmi argues in *The Colonizer and the Colonized* that "colonized society is a diseased society in which internal dynamics no longer succeed in creating new structures."[34] Without a dynamic social system, the colonised society is unable to adapt to intergenerational conflict. It hardens into "a mask under which it slowly smothers and dies."[35] The distorted breathing patterns of the family, in this analytic, are symptom of "a dying colonialism": a succession of smothering situations that may be diagnosed as the problems of the colonised society. But taking such a schematic approach to combat breathing fails to address the dynamic role that breathing plays in the novel, since it is not simply the passive indicator of underlying distortions; the presentation of distorted breathing is, like other forms of mimicry, "at once resemblance and menace."[36] But no adequate reading of the novel could take it to be a passive narrative of colonial subjugation, given how complicit the Zogoiby family and their antecedents, the Da Gamas, are with the colonial and postcolonial economic structures that bring about this systemic breathlessness.

As the novel opens, the family business, the pepper trade, is given as a root cause of colonialism, "what brought Vasco da Gama's tall ships across the ocean," "for if it had not been for peppercorns, then what is ending now in East and West might never have begun" (*MLS* 4). As Matthew Henry convincingly demonstrates, the economic successes and setbacks of the family are often set against the backdrop of major political periods, like the Indian Independence Movement, Indira Gandhi's Emergency Rule and the rise of Hindu nationalism (parodied in the novel as "Mumbai's Axis").[37] Indeed, the fortunes of the family rise and fall by the vicissitudes of the spice market, and, later, the building industry and the sex trade. Art, both that represented in the novel and the novel itself, is rendered complicit with this long history of exploitation. Rushdie contrasts the foregrounding of an "Epico-Mythico-Tragico-Comico-Super-Sexy-High-Masala-Art" to the existence of the poor and undocumented "invisible" workers in Bombay. These workers are responsible for a city invisible to public scrutiny (i.e. not seen by building code inspectors). Together, workers and city form the hidden side of a palimpsest: "Under World beneath Over world, black market beneath white; ... the whole of life was like this ... an invisible reality moved phantomwise beneath a visible fiction, subverting all its meanings" (*MLS* 184). A more complex analytic of the novel would address this complicity as an example of that "rationally pursued mutilation" that occurs when colonialism "settles" in the centre of the individual.

Again, there are correspondences between this reading and the novel's treatment of breath. Breathing in the family's spice precipitates allergic responses in Great-Grandmother Epifania, who is happier spending money than developing the business that earns it, in a satiric separation of capital from the concrete conditions of its production. Epifania's allergies set up a dialectic between the abstract conditions of colonial capital and its concrete, "breathed" experience. But they also imply a formation, as postcolonial breathlessness turns into combat breathing. Inherent in Epifania's distress are two distinct time periods: the moment of crisis (the allergic attack) and the formation of a response (her anticipation of further attacks). Thus, Epifania's allergic reaction to spice leads her to the decision to invest in perfume. Epifania's sneezing is the result of her breathing the family's spices in through her nose: "good perfume take the place of these stuffs [the spice] that maddofy my nose" (*MLS* 35). The first financial disaster for the Da Gama family foments as a result of her desire to replace the spice business with perfume. This is only the first time that breath (and allergies) will develop a politics that in turn dictates the economic decisions of the Da Gamas and the Zogoibys, in the formation of "combat breathing."

Insofar as it gathers together subjects, environments and activities, the novel uses breath as a conceit that extends beyond the body. Breath, in this sense, stands for other issues raised by the novel, rather than for, or only for, itself. Combat breathing "substitutes" for a generalised response to colonial rule. But it also describes the specific, physical manifestation of colonial distortions. Breath, always already a transient, ephemeral experience, collapses together a complex array of social, political and cultural conditions with a highly specific physiological response to these conditions. The consequence of conflation, for the wider project on breath and literature, is that combat breathing becomes a point of tense metaphoric connection between the internal, somatic conditions of postcolonial subjects and the external, fraught environments they inhabit.

The consequence might simply be that somatic modes of awareness inevitably give rise to a problematic politics of culture. Laoyene, in a sense, anticipates the cultural aspect of my argument, since he shows how Rushdie criticises the political naiveté that might use a complex political occurrence like the *convivencia* to allegorise an anodyne paradigm of multiculturalism. Laoyene's conclusions about multicultural bodies, based, like mine, on the Abraham-Boabdil hybrid, do not ultimately draw on somatic effects; in fact, the real of the body barely features in Laoyene's essay.[38] Even the sophisticated intertextual accounts that make passing reference to the breathless body, like Alberto Fernandez Carbajal's *Compromise and Resistance*, fall short of examining the body as anything more than a symptom of something else.[39] Breath does not need to be "diagnosed" as a subjective phenomenological formulation of a more objective reality, be it political (Laoyene), economic (Henry) or literary (Carbajal). If anything, it is breathlessness that forms a more objective reality for the novel, since the hallucinatory variations of the political, the economic and the artistic will depend, at some point, on the deformations of people's breathing. In order to understand the politics inherent in Rushdie's literary mode of breath awareness, as a system of signs including both the sustained deformations of "combat breathing" and the more immediate "political breathlessness," we can return once again to Abraham's asthma attack. The asthma attack does link lives, though this link is only superficially to be found between Abraham and Boabdil. In fact, it quilts Abraham together with individuals from across the whole Da Gama/Zogoiby clans, whose various breathing ailments commit the novel to a chain of respiratory signification. Asthma, argues François-Bernard Michel in *La souffle coupé*, is characterised by moments of "crisis," in which the otherwise healthy subject becomes temporarily ill.[40] Asthma throws the "normal" dichotomy between the normal and the pathological into disarray, since, for the asthmatic not in crisis, illness is absent as bodily experience, while remaining present as a source of anxiety or concern. It is, in other words, latent.[41]

Asthmatic latency links together what might be regarded as the novel's symptoms: the sighs and allergies that I have already discussed in relation to political and the economic concerns have an underlying somatic order, when read alongside the familial asthma. But, to read asthmatic latency as simply symptomatic of more material conditions ignores the discursive regimes in which breath acts as a sign: the way in which the sighs and allergies index existential anxieties in response to political troubles "in the air." And yet, these are still terms that mediate our experience of reading a novel, rather than either the immediate physiological experience of breathlessness or the more systemic conditions of "combat breathing."

References to breath in the novel are, after all, signs, rather than actual embodied conditions. More specifically, breath terms can be taken as signs that directly refer to felt concerns about invisibility and transience in the postcolony, for which politics, economics and intertextuality are reified abstractions. In order to develop this interventionist reading of breath, I want to turn towards breath's linguistic features in *The Moor's Last Sigh*, namely catachresis and markedness. Then, I show how these features contribute to an implicit critique of a purely biopolitical understanding of combat breathing.

These features are evident in a particularly contained way in a page and a half meditation, where Moraes Zogoiby enumerates a plethora of breath significances. The meditation, which begins "in my family we've always found the world's air hard to breathe," interrupts the narrative at a climactic moment: the narrator's maternal grandmother, Isabella, has just died of a combination of tuberculosis and lung cancer (*MLS* 53). By transferring the focus from Isabella's cough to "the world's air," Moraes displaces the family's "breathing problems" to a broader social epistemic atmosphere (*MLS* 53). The failure of the body interfaces with the failure of the air, already understood to be "Life's Last Gasp Saloon," or "the Ultimo Suspiro gas station" (*MLS* 4). Yet, immediately, "a sigh isn't just a sigh. We inhale the world and breathe out meaning" (*MLS* 54). On a physiological level, this might refer to the sense of ease the asthmatic feels when she is finally able to exhale. Yet it also implies that a chaotic jumble of sense-data ("the world") is, through the process of breathing, ordered and made meaningful. The relationship between individual and world is not a matter of thought, but of breath, transformation and meaning-making. For Rushdie's asthmatic, breath twins the vulnerability and resilience of the postcolonial subject.

The respiratory permutations of this meditation pull at a number of different traditions: physiological, literary, philosophical and etymological (*MLS* 53–54). Moraes will draw on all these traditions to consider what it means to become one's breath in a moment of asthmatic crisis. So, he notes, "such force of self as I retain focuses upon the faulty operations of my chest: the coughing, the fishy gulps" (*MLS* 53). "It is not thinking makes us so," he gently chides Shakespeare's Hamlet, "but air." "*Suspiro ergo sum*. I sigh therefore I am," he utters in playful homage to Descartes. "The Latin as usual tells the truth: *suspirare* = *sub*, below, +*spirare*, verb, to breathe. *Suspiro*: I under-breathe" (*MLS* 53). The Latin, of course, does not tell the truth, nor does it follow that Rushdie's playful reworking of Shakespeare or Descartes is much more than a baroque elaboration. But the meditation does highlight formal features and functions of breath explored in the novel, which cut across philosophical, literary, physiological and etymological disciplines. Collectively, these formal features, when read across their disciplinary divisions, anticipate the observation that breath is divided, across disciplines, into aesthetic and biopolitical functions

Breath replaces thinking as the first principle of Moraes's sceptical philosophy. If Descartes began from the principle that, in order to doubt, he must think, and therefore be, Moraes begins from the more playful assumption that, since air is what makes us so, his sighing is proof that he exists. This may be a reference to embodiment; more likely, however, we read it as an allusion to the novel's title. This is, after all, Moraes's (the Moor's) last sigh. The metatextual reference is to Moraes's self-identification as a textual construct, whose "being" is entirely bound up in narrating the text (sighing). But breath is a particularly unreliable first principle, since its referent slips easily between bodily function and aerious substance. In Moraes's meditation, the slippage develops between four distinct, discursive practices: physiology, literature, philosophy and etymology. The result is catachresis, or, what Jacques Derrida has called "the violent and forced abusive inscription of a sign, the imposition of a sign upon a meaning which did not yet have its own proper sign in language."[42] Breath, the violent sign, imposes itself on breathing in its heterodox meanings as physical process, poetic expression, philosophical principle and etymological elucidation. Breath is catachrestic because it imposes a generic sign onto a heterodox series of protocols connected by little more than a metaphoric connection to human respiration. This has political ramifications, particularly for postcolonialism, as

Gayatri Spivak observes when she invokes catachresis as a political means for "reversing, displacing, and seizing the apparatus of value-coding."[43] In this light, Moraes's suggestion that "we inhale the world and breathe out meaning" becomes altogether more sinister. The meaning that Moraes breathes out in his *Sigh* imposes on his references to Descartes and Shakespeare the collective sense of a postcolonial subjectivity that, perhaps, yields darker implications when associated with the structural manipulations of Abraham's criminal empire.

The different registers of breath "breathe out" not altogether compatible meanings. These incompatibilities are emphasised because Rushdie compresses them into a single paragraph. *The Moor's Last Sigh* marks breath as much in its differences as its repetition. Therefore, if breath is catachrestic, eliding or violating different conceptual registers, it is also "marked." The net effect of both the differences, or inconsistencies, and the repetitions, or continuities, is to emphasise breath or mark it. In the introduction to this volume, we discussed "marking," those phonological, grammatical or semantic features that distinguish the particular iteration of a word from its dominant, "default" meaning. By asserting its deviation from the norm, marking grants the marked term a conceptual significance. Deviation may be measured through consistencies or inconsistencies, but it must emerge in context.

Contextual deviation has wider implications for studies of the novel genre. My underlying generic assumption is that breath, in novels, intensifies what Frederic Jameson has called "the antinomies of realism."[44] Since novels have no need to mention that characters breathe, any mention of breath necessarily contributes either to the novel's "destiny" (the narrative message) or its "affect" (the concerns of its narration).[45] Breath contributes to the narrative or the description, but it functions as neither a narrative device nor a descriptive detour. This link between world and subjective experience has important consequences for thinking postcolonial subject–space relations, which I will turn to in due course. Not being necessary or optimal for concision or meaning, a "superfluous" mention of breath must therefore designate an emphasis. This assertion relies on a structuralist understanding of breath: it may be taken as an arbitrary sign, whose referent is marked by virtue of unusual semantic or syntactic activity. But it is worth recalling a further aspect of our earlier discussion of markedness. Markedness originates as a biological reference to normal breathing patterns in Trubetzkoy's *Principles of Phonology*: "In any correlation based on the manner of overcoming an obstruction a 'natural' absence of marking is attributable to that opposition member whose production requires the least deviation from normal breathing. The opposing member is then of course the marked member."[46]

Trubetzkoy's use of "normal breathing" as an index should provoke readers of *The Moor's Last Sigh*, not least because all breathing is somewhat abnormal in the novel. This extends from the unhealthy narrator, Moraes, who focuses "upon the faulty operations of my chest" to the bodyguard, Sammy Hazaré, whose lack of "breathing problems" itself implies an abnormal lung capacity: he wins "impromptu lung-power contests (holding of breath, blowing of a tiny dart through a long metal blowpipe, extinguishing of candles)" (*MLS* 53; 312). If the "normal" is unmarked, it tacitly promotes a standard rhythm and volume for breath, against which any variation may be measured. Moraes's standard, however, is recognisably "faulty"; it deviates, but from what? Clearly, norms are being challenged here, but first we should consider briefly which norms these might be. Breath has two significant "normalities" that work in quite different, even contradictory, ways: aesthetic symmetry and physiological function.

Aesthetically, breath is often understood to be a symmetrical cycle of inhalation and exhalation. For example, Samuel Beckett's *Breath*, the 35-second performance piece that fades in and out over a stage covered in rubbish, turns the inhalation and exhalation of a single breath into a symmetrical procedure.[47] Beckett allots inhalation and exhalation equal time and sound intensity, despite there being little physiological basis for this correspondence. *Breath*'s stage directions suggest the symmetrical inhalation and exhalation should each be associated with a cry, or "vagitus." These first and last cries are present, equally symmetrically, in *The Moor's Last Sigh*. Moraes will say of himself: "I am what began long ago with an exhaled cry, what will conclude when a glass held to my lips remains clear" (*MLS* 53). Later, we find that Moraes actually gives forth a "vagitus uterinus," or first cry in utero: "I ... unleashed a mighty groan" as Aurora hears "my first sound emerging from inside her body" (*MLS* 145). Yet again, he truncates his life cycle to phono-aesthetic symmetry: "From Moo to Moor, from first groan to last sigh: on such hooks hang my tales" (*MLS* 145). While *Breath* alienates the aesthetics of respiration from its physiological basis by making it wholly symmetrical, Rushdie attempts something more complicated. After all, Rushdie's breath, as the aesthetic focus of an art object, is not wholly symmetrical: "it is easier to breathe in than out," Moraes tells us (*MLS* 53).

In *The Moor's Last Sigh*, aesthetic symmetries and physiological exigencies of breath coalesce into a normative practice. In many ways, their tension maps imperfectly on to the tension that Aurora Zogoiby, Moraes's mother, experiences in her artwork, post-Independence: "the tension between Vasco Miranda's playful influence, his fondness for imaginary worlds whose only natural law was his own sovereign whimsicality, and Abraham's dogmatic insistence on the importance ... of a clear-sighted naturalism that would help India describe herself to herself" (*MLS* 173). Rushdie's implicit challenge here is to ways in which aesthetic play and physiological naturalism both ultimately prioritise problematic normative practices.

In order to unpick the normativity implied in breath, it is worth thinking about how a supposedly apolitical physiology may be just as ideologically marked as any form of aesthetic symmetry. Here, we have a precedent in Lundy Braun's excellent *Breathing Race into the Machine: The Surprising Career of the Spirometer from Plantation to Genetics*.[48] Braun addresses the problematic ways in which spirometry was used to naturalise racial distinctions in medical practice. At least some of the standard measures used in spirometry, Braun argues, occlude a deeply troubling racial history, where the normalised practice of "correcting" for ethnic grouping forgets its origins in slave plantations and indentured service. Breath science has a biopolitical edge with consequences for the whole notion of normal breathing as physiological function. If "normal breathing" is a contested site, the biological basis of Trubetzkoy's markedness is necessarily suspected. Although work in linguistics has recognised these problems and moved on from Trubetzkoy (not least through Joseph Greenberg's work on frequency), biologically based markedness still has conceptual value in thinking about breath. It just requires a two-stage approach. First, the deviation ("the marked term") is noted, and then, second, the norm ("the unmarked term") is assessed for the ideological baggage it carries. In thinking about this play between markedness and unmarkedness, alongside the immediacy of postcolonial breathlessness and the more protracted problems of combat breathing, Braun's biopolitical concerns clarify why breath is a sign, rather than a symptom, of political, economic and, in the novel, literary control. If breath was a symptom, it would simply point to the underlying, "real" conditions of the novel, whether political or economic or cultural. But, in a real sense, these conditions are formed in response to and in concert with somatic effects that morph and change over time.

Earlier, we found Rushdie's nasal anomalies to be the more marked when set against Gandhi's hygiene norms. This might be the basis for a further, symptomatic reading, in which a comparative reading of Gandhi and Rushdie might diagnose in the ills of the nose a symptom of the nation's ills. But it seems more pertinent to return to my discussion of Gandhi, via the subsequent observations in this chapter: that the acute crisis of postcolonial breathlessness can deform itself into an extended period of "combat breathing"; that exercising a symptomology of breath may well hasten, rather than hinder, this process of deformation; that the catachretic qualities of breath, as a term with multiple, conflicting meanings, may contribute to this deformation; and that Rushdie highlights some of these effects by "marking" breath's normativity. The consequence, then, of reading *The Moor's Last Sigh* alongside *A Guide to Health* is nothing less than a deconstruction of a breath-related postcolonial politics. If the anticolonial gesture is to disrupt the pervasive effects of combat breathing, by instantiating new, "healthier" regulations for physiologies, the obvious point of concern for the postcolonial critic is the striking resemblance new regulations bear to colonial-era policies.[49] Breath patterns may have immediate deformities, whether in the asthmatic crisis or the nasal blockage. But when these deformities are systematised, as regulatory conditions whose distortions are interpolated by breathing subjects, mere resolution of the individual crisis or blockage will no longer suffice. Indeed, "resolving" the problem, in its acute phase, may well occlude precisely those systemic problems that Rushdie's breath metaphors help disclose. If the need for actual medical attention in actual moments of respiratory distress appears to offer compelling reasons to dismiss this "systemic critique" as a luxury of the fit and the well, we must remember that combat breathing offers not just the rallying cry it became, but a warning against such language, which, all too easily, collapses distinctions between actual, suffering bodies and their mobilisation for political purposes. What Rushdie ultimately offers us is not a resolution for the problem of combat breathing. Rather, he reminds us that subjects who breathe will always be mediated through a language more attentive to breath's poetic significances than the mundanity that attends each individual, unmarked breath.

Notes

1. See Black Lives Matter (2016). For Christina Sharpe's account of Eric Garner, breath and "wake work," see Sharpe (2016, 112–117). On the matter of the postcolony, Mbembe (2001) remains seminal.

2. Tremblay (2016), Medina (2003, 20).
3. Crawley (2016).
4. Ibid., 2.
5. Tremblay (2016).
6. Fanon (1967, 201).
7. Tremblay (2016).
8. Rushdie (1996). Hereafter *MLS*.
9. Rushdie (2012, 307).
10. Csordas (1993, 138).
11. Ibid.
12. See, for instance, Hillman and Maude (2015).
13. Bhabha (2004, 4).
14. Laoyene (2007, 145).
15. Ibid., 157.
16. Laoyene (2007, 160).
17. Fanon (1965, 65), Tremblay (2016).
18. For scholarly responses to combat breathing, see Perera and Pugliese's special issue in *Somatechnics* (2011).
19. On Rushdie's well documented feelings about Mahatma Gandhi, see Rushdie (1992).
20. Alter (2000, 31).
21. Prasad (2015, 49).
22. Jack (1956, 256).
23. Rushdie (1995, 213).
24. Gandhi (1921, 10).
25. Ibid., 13.
26. Ibid., 21.
27. Ibid.
28. Prasad (2015).
29. Douglas (2002, 36).
30. Dürr and Jaffe demonstrate how this needs to be qualified against the obvious biomedical consequences of dirt: "While pollution is in many ways a cultural construct, it is simultaneously an 'objective', quantifiable phenomenon that impacts negatively on human and ecological health" (2010, 5).
31. Viney (2014, 2).
32. Herman (2013, 1).
33. Fanon (1965, 65).
34. Memmi (2003, 143).
35. Ibid.
36. Bhabha (2004, 123).
37. Henry (2015).

38. Goodman (2018) notes a lacuna around medicine and health in Rushdie criticism. Goodman's focus is on alcoholism and *Midnight's Children*, but I see our projects as similarly engaged with Rushdie's choice "to interrogate the legacy of Empire through a medical lens" (309). "Combat breathing," as I theorize it, connects the systemic critique of empire that was the staple of earlier responses to Rushdie with Goodman's history of medicine critique.
39. Carbajal (2014).
40. Michel (1984, 3). See also Janssens et al. (2009); von Leupoldt et al. (2006).
41. On latency and *Stimmung*, or "atmosphere," see Gumbrecht (2012, 2013).
42. Derrida (1982, 255).
43. Spivak (1990, 228).
44. Jameson (2013).
45. Ibid., 19.
46. Trubetzkoy (1969, 146).
47. Beckett (1984, 211).
48. Braun (2014).
49. See Henry (2015).

References

Alter, Joseph S. 2000. *Gandhi's Body: Sex, Diet, and the Politics of Nationalism*. Philadelphia: Pennsylvania University Press.

Bhabha, Homi. 2004 [1994]. *The Location of Culture*. London: Routledge.

Black Lives Matter. 2016. *Guiding Principles: We Affirm That All Black Lives Matter*. http://blacklivesmatter.com/guiding-principles. Accessed 4 Apr 2016.

Braun, Lundy. 2014. *Breathing Race into the Machine: The Surprising Career of the Spirometer from Plantation to Genetics*. Minneapolis: University of Minnesota Press.

Beckett, Samuel. 1984. *Collected Shorter Plays of Samuel Beckett*. London: Faber and Faber.

Carbajal, Alberto Fernandez. 2014. *Compromise and Resistance in Postcolonial Writing: E. M. Forster's Legacy*. London: Palgrave Macmillan.

Crawley, Ashon T. 2016. *Blackpentecostal Breath: The Aesthetics of Possibility*. New York: Fordham University Press.

Csordas, Thomas. 1993. Somatic Modes of Attention. *Cultural Anthropology* 8 (2): 135–156.

Derrida, Jacques. 1982. *Margins of Philosophy*, trans. Alan Bass. Brighton: Harvester Press.

Douglas, Mary. 2002 [1966]. *Purity and Danger: An Analysis of Concepts of Pollution and the Taboo*. London: Routledge.
Dürr, Eveline, and Rivke Jaffe (eds.). 2010. *Urban Pollution: Cultural Meanings, Social Practices*. New York: Berghahn.
Fanon, Frantz. 1965. *A Dying Colonialism*, trans. Haakon Chevalier, intro. Adolfo Gilly. New York: Grove Press.
Fanon, Frantz. 1967. *Black Skins, White Masks*, trans. Charles Lam Markmann. New York: Grove Press.
Gandhi, Mahatma (Mohandas). 1921. *A Guide to Health*, trans. A. Rama Iyer. Madras: S. Ganesan.
Goodman, Sam. 2018. "Ain't It a Ripping Night": Alcoholism and the Legacies of Empire in Salman Rushdie's *Midnight's Children*. *English Studies* 99 (3): 307–324.
Gumbrecht, Hans Ulrich. 2012. *Atmosphere, Mood, Stimmung: On a Hidden Potential in Literature*, trans. Erik Butler. Stanford: Stanford University Press.
Gumbrecht, Hans Ulrich. 2013. *After 1945: Latency as Origin of the Present*. Stanford: Stanford University Press.
Henry, Matthew. 2015. Neoliberalism's Children: India's Economy, Wageless Life, and Organized Crime in *The Moor's Last Sigh*. *Ariel* 46 (3): 137–163.
Herman, James P. 2013. Neural Control of Chronic Stress Adaptation. *Frontiers in Behavioural Neuroscience* 7 (61). https://doi.org/10.3389/fnbeh.2013.00061.
Hillman, David, and Ulrike Maude. 2015. *The Cambridge Companion to the Body in Literature*. Cambridge: Cambridge University Press.
Jack, Homer Alexander. 1956. *The Gandhi Reader: A Sourcebook of His Life and Writings*. London: Penguin.
Jameson, Fredric. 2013. *The Antinomies of Realism*. London: Verso.
Janssens, Thomas, Geert Verleden, Steven De Peuter, Ilse Van Diest, and Omer Van den Bergh. 2009. Inaccurate Perception of Asthma Symptoms: A Cognitive-Affective Framework and Implications for Asthma Treatment. *Clinical Psychology Review* 29 (4): 317–327.
Laoyene, Atef. 2007. Andalusian Poetics: Rushdie's *The Moor's Last Sigh* and the Limits of Hybridity. *Ariel* 38 (4): 143–165.
Mbembe, Achille. 2001. *On the Postcolony*. Berkeley: University of California Press.
Medina, Tony. 2003. *Committed to Breathing*. Chicago: Third World Press.
Memmi, Albert. 2003 [1957]. *The Colonizer and the Colonized*, trans. Howard Greenfeld, intro. Jean-Paul Sartre, new intro. Nadine Gordimer. London: Earthscan Publications.
Michel, François-Bernard. 1984. *Le souffle coupé: Respirer et écrire*. Paris: Gallimard.
Perera, Suvendrini, and Joseph Pugliese. 2011. Combat Breathing: State Violence and the Body in Question. *Somatechnics* 1 (1): 1–14.

Prasad, Srirupa. 2015. *Cultural Politics of Hygiene in India, 1890–1940: Contagions of Feeling*. London: Palgrave Macmillan.
Rushdie, Salman. 1992 [1991]. *Imaginary Homelands: Essays & Criticism 1981–1991*. London: Vintage.
Rushdie, Salman. 1995 [1981]. *Midnight's Children*. London: Vintage.
Rushdie, Salman. 1996 [1995]. *The Moor's Last Sigh*. London: Vintage.
Rushdie, Salman. 2012. *Joseph Anton: A Memoir*. London: Jonathan Cape.
Sharpe, Christina. 2016. *In the Wake: On Blackness and Being*. Durham: Duke University Press.
Spivak, Gayatri. 1990. Poststructuralism, Marginality, Postcoloniality and Value. In *Literary Theory Today*, ed. Peter Collier and Helga Geyer-Ryan, 219–244. London: Polity Press.
Tremblay, Jean-Thomas. 2016. *Being Black and Breathing: On Blackpentecostal Breath*. LA Review of Books. https://lareviewofbooks.org/article/being-black-and-breathing-on-blackpentecostal-breath. Accessed 3 May 2018.
Trubetzkoy, N.S. 1969. *Principles of Phonology*, trans. Christiane A.M. Baltaxe. Berkeley and Los Angeles: University of California Press.
Viney, Will. 2014. *Waste: A Philosophy of Things*. London: Bloomsbury Academic.
Von Leupoldt, Andreas, Frank Riedel, and Bernhard Dahme. 2006. The Impact of Emotions on the Perception of Dyspnea in Pediatric Asthma. *Psychophysiology* 43 (6): 641–644.

Open Access This chapter is licensed under the terms of the Creative Commons Attribution 4.0 International License (http://creativecommons.org/licenses/by/4.0/), which permits use, sharing, adaptation, distribution and reproduction in any medium or format, as long as you give appropriate credit to the original author(s) and the source, provide a link to the Creative Commons license and indicate if changes were made.

The images or other third party material in this chapter are included in the chapter's Creative Commons license, unless indicated otherwise in a credit line to the material. If material is not included in the chapte's Creative Commons license and your intended use is not permitted by statutory regulation or exceeds the permitted use, you will need to obtain permission directly from the copyright holder.

The manufacturer's authorised representative in the EU is Springer Nature Customer Service Centre GmbH, Europaplatz 3, 69115 Heidelberg, Germany. If you have any concerns regarding our products, please contact ProductSafety@springernature.com

Printed and bound by CPI Group (UK) Ltd, Croydon, CR0 4YY
23/03/2026
02076447-0009